I'll Be Watching *you*

EVA MARKS

Copyright © 2023 by Eva Marks

All rights reserved.

No part of this publication may be reproduced, distributed, or transmitted in any form or by any means, including photocopying, recording, or other electronic or mechanical methods, without the prior written permission of the publisher, except as permitted by U.S. copyright law. For permission requests, contact authorevamarks@gmail.com

The story, all names, characters, and incidents portrayed in this production are fictitious. No identification with actual persons (living or deceased), places, buildings, and products is intended or should be inferred.

Book Cover by Eva Marks

A Note from the Author

I'll Be Watching You is a steamy voyeur romance, containing explicit and graphic scenes and kinks intended for mature audiences only.

Trigger and Content Warnings

Voyeur and slightly stalker tendencies by the hero, heroine is an exhibitionist who works as a sexy vlogger+podcaster, Consensual Non-Consent role play, light BDSM, Daddy kink, a very dirty use of a lab timer, adult toys, age gap, bondage, praise & degradation, dirty talking hero, spitting, attempted rape (not by the hero), back-hole play, self-pleasuring, touch her and you-stop-breathing vibes.

Continue at your own risk, and be prepared to never look at your neighbor's window the same way…

About the Book

**She doesn't know it yet, but I'll be watching.
And she *will* be mine...**

I'm a scientist. I work in a pharmaceutical company, finding cures and helping others.
At least that's what I do in the daytime...
At nights, in the darkness of my home, I'm a voyeur. But I don't just watch anyone. I watch *her*. Just *her*.
Sloane is my complete opposite. She doesn't do *anything* in the shadows. She's an exhibitionist—a performer. I've been stalking her podcast for two years.
I'm also her new neighbor...with a view into her apartment.
Being so close and not being able to touch her is torture. I want her so much it hurts. I *need* her.

And I'm *done* with just watching.

I'm coming for you, Sloane. Ready or not...

PROLOGUE
Emmanuel

Manhattan's fall holds its own kind of dark magic.

Masses of leaves in red and orange hues paint the town in all shades of earth-tone colors. They appear on the trees first, the branches billowing in the early winds of the season resembling a fire coursing through the streets, predicting the chaos of the nearing winter.

When they fall on the sidewalk, before being cleared out, their semblance of blood drops on the gray stones reminds me of something sinister.

And in this clandestine atmosphere, that's where I thrive.

That's why I've grown to love this season above all else during the ten years I've been a New Yorker, and I've observed the four of them closely.

Just as I take note of the boutique stores, bars, and restaurants decorating the street of my new

I'll Be Watching You

apartment in SoHo on my way home from work. Of the tourists speaking in varying languages, neighbors contemplating the meaning behind their existence, their art, the climate.

I see it all. I never engage.

Because that's what I do.

I watch.

As a scientist for the past two decades, I've been studying the findings my lab experiments produce since I was a sixteen-year-old in high school. My profession imprinted in me those learning patterns, where opening my eyes to wonder about my surroundings and analyzing them has become second nature.

But my driven need to look isn't limited to inanimate objects or any random passerby.

No. It reaches far past that. It's the vice I live with, the burden I carry, the secret I mask behind a successful career and a somber expression.

I'm a voyeur.

And it's that kind of sickness that I plan on feeding tonight.

The renovated elevator takes me up to the top floor, the third where I live. I don't bother switching the lights on when the doors open to the dark hallway.

Though I have to reach the end of the narrow passageway to my apartment door, I prefer walking in the shadows. Better than being the object a nosy neighbor might glare at through their peephole.

It's not like I'm paranoid. But if anyone's going to be doing the looking, it's me.

My keys to the lab, my apartment building, and my home clink on the keychain when I fish them out of my shoulder bag where I keep my laptop.

Both travel with me wherever I go, always, unless it's a short trip downstairs, which is why I have a safe installed at home. They hold my secrets guarded against the outside world, the ones of GeneOrg, my workplace, along with the personal ones that'd get me fired and cast out of society as if I were a criminal.

I've gone to lengths to ensure I wouldn't be. I've been aware of tendencies ever since the urge to see overtook me like a storm as a teenager, and I have been trying to blend into society without letting my sickness bleed out of its confinements.

I've done everything in my power to respect women's privacy, to only peep at women who consent to it. Thanks to the internet and the wonderful free market concept of supply and demand, I lurk on the willing ones.

Women who record podcasts or videos or live streams of them prancing around their homes or having sex or reenacting this scene or the other.

Or better yet, for the past two years, *one*.

I'll Be Watching You

I open the door to my small kingdom, the haven I escape to where I can act on my deepest, darkest desires. The modern table lamp I have on the console where I dump my keys emanates a soft, low glow.

It doesn't light up the open kitchen and the living room, but it's enough for me to navigate to the table below the window.

My private, obscure corner behind rolled-down drapes.

No one would point a finger at me here, call me a freak, a thirty-six-year-old successful man who's incapable of asking a woman out.

The ruler of my kingdom, preparing to meet my woman.

Sitting down in the chair at the window, I fire up my laptop. A Band-Aid, whiskey, and a clean tumbler are already set neatly on my desk. I arranged them the way I liked it this morning so my flow isn't interrupted, so I can just act on my desires without overthinking what I'm doing and just proceed to follow the steps I repeat every time.

First, I attend to the webcam of my laptop, sealing both it and the secret aspect of my life. The blue of my eyes in my moments of weakness and perversion is mine alone.

Second, I pour myself three fingers of the drink to give me the final push, to relieve me from the constraints of the inhibitions I know I should possess.

Eva Marks

The amber liquid sloshes around in my glass as I swirl it around. Using my other hand, I click on the link to her website.

Seraphine Mallory.

My dick grows painfully hard imagining the cadence of her voice even before I press play, tempting yet unassuming. Vibrant and desirable while managing to still sound attainable, within reach for her pack of voyeurs.

Knowing others jerk off to her doesn't bother me, doesn't make me think less of her. It's her job, her talent. On the contrary, my admiration for her is endless for putting herself out there. She's never shown her face, but she reveals plenty, more than I, a person in the shadows, could ever dream of.

And with that final thought, I pull up the episode I've been craving today, letting her voice fill the void in my apartment.

"The nights have been colder, the subtle hints of winter becoming more prominent. October flew by too fast. Did you feel it, too?"

To her sensual sigh, I gulp the last of my drink.

"However, my fridge doesn't care about the weather outside. So, on this cold November day, I had to jog from the grocery store. Two minutes inside the store was all it took for the sky to break and that's when I heard those little drops of rain pelting against the store's awning."

I'll Be Watching You

I open the fly of my sage-green slacks, relaxing in my chair as I free my thick erection from my boxer briefs.

"See, despite the cold, the sun was out when I went outside, but the bad, bad weather tricked me. I looked outside, horrified, then back at my white T-shirt, realizing it wouldn't survive the trip home…"

My eyes close, picturing this little woman stressed out about her shirt about to be drenched soon, wondering if she had a bra on. In the slow rubs of my cock, I see myself beside her on the dairy aisle, noticing her distress, considering whether I should offer her my help.

I want to. Fuck, do I need to come harder, knowing I could look. That I could've maybe approached her…

"It left me no choice but to make a run for it once the cashier rang up my milk."

I groan, feeling my balls tighten and my dick swell. Every time I hear her say *milk,* I lose myself a little more, aching for her pussy to squeeze my cock dry. I won't do it, I'm incapable of that kind of intimacy, but if I'd ever risk being someone else, it'd be for her.

"As I was jogging with my head bent low, a sense of someone turning their head and watching overcame me. I clutched my breasts, trying to get them to stop bouncing."

Like the man I wanted to be in the grocery store, I wanted to be that guy in the street. I picture myself standing in an alley wearing my raincoat, eying her from the shadows.

"Finally, though, alone, I made it home. Wet…"

I stroke faster, seeing myself as the hero who would've carried her to safety.

"…breathless…"

Precum dampens my thumb, my hips jutting forward, my dick pulsing in my palm.

"…and in the privacy of my home, at last, I was free to take off everything and protect myself from the cold in a hot bath."

"Christ," I grunt as my orgasm pummels through me, and sperm coats my fingers.

I come so hard my chair grates back from the sheer force of it.

She does this to me.

The woman who isn't mine to want.

The woman who is in my dreams, who is mine and mine alone.

My Seraphine.

CHAPTER ONE
Sloane

"Ugh, talk about a nightmare." I collapse on my couch, my forearm covering my face. "A bra at home or having the drapes closed all day? Being shackled to my radiator would've been less of a punishment than *this*."

The eye roll of my best friend, Liberty, is practically audible on the other side of the phone. "Oh, please, you're a great actress but I'd appreciate it if you cut back on Macbeth where it's not needed."

"Easy for you to say." I match her most-likely-there eye roll, then raise it by adding an exasperated sigh. "Not all of us can be shielded by one-way window films on the fortieth floor uptown."

I'm not jealous, I'm just telling it like it is. She lives in the Upper East Side, Manhattan, married to the equivalent of media royalty, in an extremely shielded apartment. Where she and her husband, Dexter, walk naked. A lot.

So, this is fact one. Fact two is, I'm happily single, renting a two-bedroom apartment in SoHo which I'm obsessed with. It's the cutest thing ever, has high ceilings and spacious rooms that far outweigh the living situation of most twenty-seven-year-olds.

The income I make as a freelancer using my voice, and sometimes a visual of my legs and torso, to people online is substantial enough to afford this place, a dream come true since I was a kid living in Queens. Now that I have it—even though it's a rental—I'm not uttering the slightest word of complaint about it.

But, and this is fact three, it's not private. There's a neighbor's window facing mine, looking into my living room. It was a nonissue with the former tenant, a woman who barely looked in my direction.

Three days ago, however, a man moved in. I have no idea who this person is, have barely gotten a sight of him, and yet I don't like this change. My job involves a hell of a lot of exhibitionism, but it isn't to say I'd like having a stranger gawking at me whenever he decides to eventually be home.

"Sloane, you're talking like you're going to have to inconvenience yourself every waking minute of the day." My friend's tone switches from friendly mocking to compassionate. She does her best to

I'll Be Watching You

encourage me, and I lower my defenses gradually to her loving voice. "I mean, just because you work from home doesn't mean he does, too. Could be he'll be out by seven in the morning, back by midnight. Party over the weekends."

"Okay, I like where this is heading." I favor sitting up for slouching, quitting my unattractive whining. I'm a grown woman, damn it. And Liberty is right. Both for opening my eyes and not letting me act like a little bitch.

Unless…

"Then again, ugh," I groan at the holes in her plan to the pounding of my unwilling conscience in my chest to shut this idea down. "Wouldn't it be the worst kind of double standard? I'll be doing what I said I would hate him to do to me. I can't. Nope. No, no, no."

"I'm not talking about stalking. I'm talking about sneaking a glance, you know, casually, out the window a few times in the morning and then in the evening. You'll have a better idea of when he's there, so he doesn't have his privacy violated. It's a win-win, really."

I wiggle my toes on my shaggy, striped, gray-blue-and-white rug, and my favorite purchase, besides my precious studio equipment. A treasure, some—aka me—might call it on those cold November nights in New York. That, combined with the boiler system in our building.

Eva Marks

Which is me stalling while actually considering peeking into someone's apartment.

"If he catches me staring, I'll feel horrible."

It dawns on me all of a sudden that I'm not only protecting myself and my affinity for the braless life. It's him, too. I don't want either of us to be uncomfortable.

"It'll be a horrible lose-lose, Lib."

"Not when he sees a gorgeous woman with thick, long reddish-brown locks and dark, almond-shaped eyes ogling him. Briefly. I mean, he'll definitely like what he sees in the window." Liberty resumes her problem-solving mode. "The question is… Do you? Is he hot?"

"I didn't have a good look." My toe goes back and forth on the rug, my cheeks heating at the memory.

"How are you sure it's a guy, then?"

"His back. That's what I saw. And his profile, for a second." The burn in my cheeks permeates to my neck, my arms. Despite not wanting to, claiming this is wrong, I did, in fact, stalk him. A little. "Then he faced forward, scratched what must've been his jaw, talked to the movers, tipped them, then poof. Went out after they did. Since then, my drapes have been closed."

With the phone tucked between my ear and shoulder, I stand up, suddenly craving tea, of all things. My crimson T-shirt rises over my belly

I'll Be Watching You

button when I stretch my limbs, grazing my navel piercing, a favorite of my subscribers.

"Details, please." Her newfound intrigue seeps into her voice. "Tell me more about that *back*."

A smirk tugs on my lips as I put the teapot on the stove. "He's not bulky in any way. Thin, but not scrawny. About six feet tall. His profile, though." I sigh dramatically to downplay it, even though in truth, other than being upset about him messing with my routine, the man has very attractive features. "Strong nose, thick eyebrows. Oh, and yeah, his stubble. He has—or had—one, and it was…nice."

"Uh, hold up. You're saying there's been a man you try—and fail—to trick me into believing is a nuisance, who's actually handsome, and you didn't…"

"Didn't what?"

"Hmm… Anything else I should know about?"

My grin widens and my laugh is uncontainable. "Aren't you supposed to be married?"

"Happily," she exclaims, the fierce, proud woman in her shining through. "To a wonderful, sweet man at that. But you're my best friend and A) He might be your one, B) This right here is living the fantasies I get from the romance novels I read, so… Spill it."

"Nope." The water boils in the teapot on the stove as I give Liberty my short answer.

"Sloane."

"Lib."

"Like I said. You're my best friend." She pauses, takes a breath, continuing. "In all seriousness, this is more for you than for me. Liking a man, any man, is a good starting point for you. I'm here as a cheerleader to encourage it."

I groan inwardly at the list of men I wish I never set my eyes on. Then I make a crack out of it.

"His back, the ridges of it, they were outlined beneath his gray fitted dress shirt," I start in my podcast voice.

"No, please, tell Seraphine to go away." Her horror is only half-assed because she starts laughing too.

And Liberty's laugh, to her detriment, encourages me to stick to it. "You don't like Seraphine? I'm offended."

"I like her plenty, but for this exercise, be my serious Sloane Ashby again if that's okay. Let's be serious about him."

"Fine, fine, here I am." The teapot shrieks at my back, a shrill sound joining our chuckles. I spin to take it off the stove and pour hot water into my mug.

The steam billows, the scent of ginger tea permeating through the apartment. During the four years of my current career, none of the other herbal teas I've tried provide the desired relief ginger has for my vocal cords.

I'll Be Watching You

I take my tea back to the couch, sitting comfortably on my feet. "He's a guy. He'll be the same. Not interested." My eyes are drawn to the contents of my mug, the tea bag lying at the bottom of it. "As liberal as the men in this city are, the ones I've dated... Well, you know."

"I'm aware you had a streak of jerk-frog kisses." Her motherly tone envelops me through the phone in a warm embrace. "The dating world sucks, that's the sad reality of it. I hear other friends being turned down for any number of reasons or worse, being ghosted."

"Gross, I hate those the most." My face scrunches and I shiver with disgust. "And still, having one man after the other telling you that doing sexy podcasts or recording myself walking around the apartment from the waist down isn't what they look for in a wife... I hate it. I'm not up to being judged by assholes *again*."

"It's their loss, Sloane, that's what it is. Fuck them."

"I don't blame them—"

"Fuck them, nonetheless," she cuts in. "Maybe this guy, showing on your sorta doorstep, is a sign. I'd hate for you to miss out on it because a handful of guys couldn't grasp what a magical woman you are, to respect you for being a badass boss lady with one of the coolest careers out there."

I sip my tea, doing something, anything, other than crying. "Weren't we laughing, like a second ago?"

"Yeah, we were. And for us to get back to that, for you to be my smiling, confident queen, I want you to see this guy's face."

"I'm not sure I'll be comfortable doing that." The spicy ginger tea tastes delicious on my tongue. A tingling comfort.

Liberty goes on, "A glimpse, one second, that's all I'm asking. You'll end up liking him? Great, bake the man cookies and prance over to the building nearby. You won't? Avoid him when he's in the apartment, close the drapes. That easy, right? Please try? For me?"

"Ugh, fine." I twist on my couch, flicking a gaze in the direction of the apartment whose windows face mine.

Through the narrow opening in the drapes, I can tell there's no light coming from his direction. There's no light outside either, so I can't imagine him just sitting there in the darkness. "He's not here, though."

"Good thing you're a night person." A smile blends into her voice, then a burst of laughter I'm sensing has nothing to do with my situation. "Dexter, stop. Not now. Oh, this? Okay, okay. I'm coming. Sloane, I have to go now."

I'll Be Watching You

"He's tempting you with your favorite red wine?"

"Indeed."

Sounds of glasses clinking on their counter, my final cue to leave. "Talk tomorrow?"

"Duh! You need to tell me *everything*."

"You mean about how you tried hooking up the unhookable?"

"I mean if you need a cookie recipe." She laughs, and this one's for me.

After we hang up, I let Liberty's idea roll around my head. It doesn't feel like breaking any neighborly boundaries. We ought to catch a glimpse of each other someday. This closed-drapes situation isn't sustainable; it isn't like me to hide. I'd die if I keep it up.

So why not make it the present moment, get it over with? I'll control my state of dress, sneak a teeny tiny glance that wouldn't disrupt any of us.

I'll tell Liberty he's not my taste, but I won't even stare long enough to see what he looks like. One glance tonight, another couple tomorrow. Nothing more, nothing less.

In return, I'll bake him a batch of cookies anyway, to ease my conscience. With the compensation in the form of chocolatey dough in my mind, my decision doesn't disturb me as much anymore.

Eva Marks

I'm an honest, decent person, I tell myself as I sit there, opening the drapes to wait until my neighbor returns from work.

CHAPTER TWO
Sloane

The time on my phone changes, eight twenty-nine becoming eight-thirty on the dot when I'm startled by the dull light switching on in the apartment across from me.

It's been an hour and a half since Liberty and I spoke. Ninety minutes of me being sprawled on the couch, losing myself in a list of articles online and forgetting about the fact that I've been waiting here for him, being a stalker without really being a stalker.

I've got caught up in studying, reading work-related articles to provide material for my podcasts to last a month.

Like how describing what color you paint your nails can contribute to a sexy scene, or that panting alone could be a real turn-on to the person on the other side getting off on envisioning whatever they wanted.

Or—and that made me confident *I* am not it—on the topic of stalking. The podcasts where I dabbled into the subject got a ton of hits, and looking for more ideas had me sucked into it.

Inspiration flowed, and my curiosity piqued. Slowly and meticulously, I began forming a full-on fantasy of a guy trailing my every move, maybe even breaking into my home like one article mentioned.

By eight-thirty in the evening, I've been deep into a well-thought-out plan about a series of episodes I could create for my people.

My job is more than the source of my livelihood—it's my passion, my platform to express myself as the actress I've dreamt about being. There, I'm a performer limited solely by her imagination and nobody else's, and loving every minute of it, too.

Hence, why the reason to explain why I've been lying here in wait completely escaped me.

Now though, with the light on in the adjacent apartment, I remember.

I very much do.

Mr. New Neighbor.

The amber glow announcing his arrival should be enough for me to start setting the limits. I should walk to the window, head bowed as if I don't even acknowledge his existence, roll them down, then go to bed.

Unfortunately, my physical reaction to him refuses to let me back off.

I'll Be Watching You

Liquid heat swarms into my stomach, slow and sensual as I scramble to the couch that faces away from the window where I fold myself deep into the cushions. Hiding.

I haven't even laid my eyes on the man's face, yet here I am, thrilled and mildly aroused at the prospect of this silent interaction.

Damn you, Liberty, for planting dirty ideas in my head.

True, the ten months I haven't dated could've caused my reaction to being on the horny side. But it still doesn't feel like a decent excuse to act ten years beneath my age. Or maybe I can blame my loneliness for it.

Or…it's due to me being the observer for a change. I'm accustomed to being on the other side of the looking glass, so this change could be what excites me, not the man.

Or, Liberty slips right inside my inner conversations again, *you're thinking he might be cute.*

I tsk, pressing the heels of my palms to my eyes. No. This isn't it, and I'll make sure to emphasize how not *it* it is the next time I talk to my best friend.

The deep breath I suck in does nothing to soothe me. The hunger remains inside me, urging me to raise my head and look. It's only a peek, a quick *Howdy, neighbor* where he's not even aware of me howdy-ing him.

Eva Marks

You'll bake for him. It should make up for this whole scene. Which he's not privy to.

The energy buzzing in my veins settles the decision for me—to go ahead and do it.

Stealthily, I slide my phone onto the gray wood coffee table. Nothing worse than to be caught holding your phone while ogling your neighbor. Once the incriminating device is out of the way, I twist on the couch, gripping the fabric of the cushions as I rise to my knees.

If he'd glance in my direction, he'll see nothing out of the ordinary. My dark hair should blend in the background, be just another shadow, and my eyes would be hardly noticeable in the distance.

Zero risk.

The living room is empty, but then I detect his shadow a second before he walks into the living room from the hallway.

Holy shit.

Holy fucking shit.

This guy's front is much hotter than the glimpse of a profile I was given three days ago.

Because, goddammit, his eyes. It's impossible to look away from those utmost sparking, brilliant, blue eyes ever known to mankind. They're so bright and large that their uniqueness comes across the distance between us.

His other features aren't half bad, either, and that's an understatement, even though I can't see

I'll Be Watching You

them as well. His shaved jaw shows off his high, defined cheekbones, and right in the middle of it sits a pair of sculpted lips. Not too full or plump, but ones I'm freaking positive have kissed many women—or men—until they were on the verge of fainting with delight.

"Beautiful," I murmur to an empty room. I'm used to it by now, seeing how I talk to myself for a living. "A tad strange, these huge eyes and prominent lips. Still, it works. I have a stunning neighbor."

Then what I feared the most happens. As soon as those whispers leave my mouth, he turns to face the window.

"Shit!" I dive down, covering my face. Like that would help.

Breathe, Sloane.

There's no chance he caught me. Couldn't have, really. A shred of a second isn't nearly enough to make out two inches of a person.

I'm safe. I'm safe.

I am safe.

But while I lie there, knees to my chest and palms on my face, I realize something. My rapid heartbeat rages in my chest for another reason than the adrenaline of being witnessed peeping into a stranger's home.

Excitement. Infatuation. The tug in my lower belly and the cold shiver running along my chest reaffirm it, spreading goosebumps in their wake. My nipples tighten, peaking under my T-shirt, little round mounds at the top of my full D-cup breasts.

The neighbor's presence permeates farther into the room when I imagine his face while I reach for the top of my breasts. Using the light touch of my palm, I stroke the aroused mounds, teasing them like I imagine he would.

My legs press together, my thighs clenching in a desperate want to relieve this growing pressure between them. I'm about to slip my hand inside my gray sweats and lose myself in the stranger's eyes and give in to pleasure and...

Then I think better of it.

Maybe... Maybe I'll record it, reenact my fantasies in the way that gets me off the most and I wouldn't be sitting here like a pervert, using the fact he's so close and somehow violating him.

Yes, that can work. I'll do it this one time, then go back to my original plan of cookies gifted, drapes closed, privacy is given.

Like Liberty said, it's a win-win.

Mr. Hot Neighbor must still be in the living room, so I lower myself to the floor on my hands and knees. Beneath the windows, protected from view by my apartment's walls, I crawl down the hallway on the heated hardwood floors.

The sensuality of the act itself puts me more into the mood than I'm bothered by the pain in my

I'll Be Watching You

knees. I do not doubt that if this man would've asked me to do that for him, what no one else had, what I would've allowed to no other, I'd have done it in a heartbeat.

Flushed and wanting, I reach the studio in my bedroom. I traverse the space on all fours, quick to jump up and roll down the drapes on the two windows facing his apartment and the larger one in the direction of the street.

Before I sit at my studio desk, I head over to my dresser where I keep my sex toys. I discovered that rubbing my clit or fucking myself with my own fingers damages the sound quality of my recordings, so they help.

And also, they're a hell of a lot of fun to play with on my own.

I pull the first drawer open, sorting between the vibrators, dildos, ropes, butt plugs, and many others. "Which of you ladies screams *Sexy neighbor*, hmm?"

They don't form a verbal answer—of course, they don't—except one does quietly call for me to choose her above all others. My wireless, silent, butterfly vibrator.

Its wings and antenna buzz in my palm as I switch it on the lowest volume button. I amp it up to its highest volume, and if the beautiful insect was a live one, this would've been the moment it would've flown beyond my reach, it flaps so hard.

Eva Marks

The buzzing sounds add another layer to my craving for the guy I've been trying desperately to avoid. I turn it off before I forfeit the magic spell of building a fantasy, carrying it with me to light a couple of my peppermint candles on the end table I have in my studio slash bedroom.

Once the atmosphere is set to my liking, I'm ready to start.

My panties are soaked with need from having those blue gorgeous eyes imprinted in my head as well as the knowledge people will listen to me moan for him, come for this man.

On two trembling feet, I tread on my shaggy rug toward my office chair, shucking off my sweats and panties. I'm a ball of desire ready to explode as I sit down, spreading my legs to position the butterfly, picturing the dirty scene starring my neighbor.

A relieved exhale brushes past my lips as I slip the vibrator in and settle into my already wet pussy. I part my swollen lips, positioning the antennas on either side of my clit, and fuck, what I wouldn't give to have *his* face down there.

After I set the butterfly to the lowest intensity, I strip off my T-shirt. The warmth of the apartment cradles my breasts, and the thrumming from between my legs begins the slow process of setting me on fire while I work around the podcasting equipment on my desk.

I'll Be Watching You

"Fuck," I mutter, leaning back in the chair with my earbuds on. I pull the arm holder of the microphone stand so it hovers inches from my lips, then place each leg on the chair's arms.

With this one final moan, I switch up the vibrator's intensity and press *record*.

"Mmm. There's such a satisfying feeling to being observed, to being preyed on. To be watched, revered, even from afar, like I was today." I start, voicing my imminent need as I let my eyes flutter shut. "God, his gaze on me was intense, following me wherever I went, and I can barely handle it anymore. By pure luck, at one of the times his attention burrowed into my head with its force, I whipped my head back to see him, caught a glimpse of those insane spring-sky blue eyes. I knew then that I hadn't been imagining things since the morning when I went on my coffee run, and I wanted to approach him with all the lust he'd woken in me, but I also knew it'd ruin our game. So, I kept on walking."

My neighbor's face slithers into the forefront of my consciousness, harder, sharper than before. I make up for the parts that were too far for me to see well, then go on to picture what it'd be like to be the subject of his glare, how he'd haunt me through the streets.

Me, Sloane. Not Seraphine. Not some other person's ideal woman. No. Just Sloane. I conjured this scenario in my head, then marched on, dutifully playing the role of Seraphine.

"I"—I moan, pinching one of my nipples. The tug and release turn a sharp bite of pain to a warm coat of pleasure—"fuck, I'm so fucking horny remembering it. But it's not my fault I'm like this."

My hungry grunt fills the air around me, permeating into the mic. "It isn't, it's *his*. He devoted the whole day to turning me on by stalking me, his gaze and attention were burning me alive, making my pussy throb."

I rub lightly, pinch and twist my nipples, placing my feet on the desk and grabbing them by the toes. Bending my knees, open and willing even though I have my butterfly and nothing else to attend to my mounting needs.

"He'd been toying with me, all over the city, like a shark circling its lunch."

The sounds rising from my throat when I amp up the vibrator to the highest speed while calling on pictures of blue eyes and lusting lips are borderline animalistic. They're new, even, to my own ears, wild and uncontrollable.

"My nipples pebbled to the point of agony under my knitted blouse when his fixation was almost palpable at the park where I had my lunch."

I feel the brush of his shoulder almost as the ghost of my stranger enters the room, crosses it to

I'll Be Watching You

stand behind me. It's like he's really here, pressing his hands to the back of my neck, almost choking me.

I gasp.

"A knot in my belly has been wound tightly, knowing this man who followed me on the way home tracked me while I stopped at the old record store."

My pussy clenches around the vibrator, juices flooding down my crack as my walls suck the butterfly in.

"Then... then he was right behind me, the heat of his fixation drilling into me, announcing his presence at every turn as I headed home."

I'm close, so freaking close. Each pant is a dire attempt to suck in a breath my tight lungs refuse me, every squeeze of my hips is a part of the battle to hold on to my orgasm a little while longer.

"All the way up to my apartment. And now I think I hear the lock being picked, he's"—moan—"letting himself"—my hips thrusting forward—"in."

The dynamite inside me is fit to detonate. I just have to hold on a little while longer, have his presence reverberate through me for a few more seconds.

"And—and—oh, my God, he's here. The floorboards creak under his boots. He's in my bedroom, striding straight ahead toward me. No, please, don't. It was all a game."

Eva Marks

My imagination runs wild. Him crawling beneath the desk, throwing away the vibrator, forcing me to lose my clothes and take me in what some might call dubious consent.

"I don't want to, fuck, don't want his lips sucking my clit, these stranger hands twisting my nipples until I cry out in pain, but I can't help but get wetter and hotter. I'm dripping all over the mouth that takes what isn't his, pushing me into"—I groan so loud the neighbors probably hear me—"an orgasm. Fuck. Fuck, fuck, fuck."

I curse and press the antennas and head of the butterfly deep into me as the most powerful climax I've ever experienced tears me from the inside like lightning cutting through the sky.

When the tremors subside and I'm fully satiated, my breath settles to its normal rhythm, my pulse returning to thrum at its low, steady pace.

I press *stop*, push away the mic, remove my headphones and let my head fall back on the back of the chair. A coat of serenity washes over me, almost as though the stranger I imagined on his knees rises to hug me and carry me to bed.

But in reality, I'm alone. Mildly disheartened, I wipe my vibrator clean, take a quick shower, and snuggle into bed.

Then I open my browser on my phone and look for the *Top 10 cookie recipes*.

I'll Be Watching You

I've been afraid of men for too long now. I think Liberty was right.

This guy might be *it*.

CHAPTER THREE
Emmanuel

It's the first Saturday that I've woken up in my new apartment. The first morning I don't have an alarm clock hammering in my ear before dawn. The first day I get to revel in the view of November's cloudy skies from this new space I now call home.

The bustling sounds from below in the street filter into the darkness that's been my reality and companion throughout my adult life. Low chatters in the café right under my window, a truck beeping while backing up, branches rustling in the wind.

There's a world out there, one that's impossible to ignore.

My mood—somber and serious as it may be—picks up. I suck in a deep breath, stretch in my bed, then get out, pulling on my olive-green sweats so I can start living too. With the apartment heated, that's really all I need.

I'll Be Watching You

Modesty isn't something I'm worried about. If the neighbor who has his or her drapes shut throughout the day and only rolled them up last night will decide to keep them there, there isn't much for him or her to see anyway. Much like all the others who've witnessed me in any state of undress, they'll be highly uninterested and move along.

The workouts I do at GeneOrg's gym are short due to the many hours I have to put in my job, and far between. Two to three fifteen-minute weight lifting workouts are hardly sufficient to grow a significant mass, resulting in my remaining defined yet unimpressive, the same as I've always been.

I'm not insecure. I'm honest. That's also why I've been on the watching side rather than being the one observed.

Especially if it means spending my rare free hours on *her*.

Although lately, I haven't had much of that either. The past six months have been brutal in the lab. We had a deadline to race toward before the competition beat us to the patent, and we slaved days and nights, workdays and weekends, over wrapping things up to make it in time.

But life or rent lease don't abide by my lab schedule. Since it ended last week, I had to hire a realtor and accept whatever suggestion fit best my list of demands.

Eva Marks

So, here I am. I get up to go to the living room to start my weekend at this place I still have to get used to calling home. The designer set the place up to my liking, decorating the living room with simplicity in mind. He set up a brown leather couch, a light round table on top of a gray rug, and a painting of a field hanging across the exposed brick wall.

The open kitchen didn't need any renovating, the gray cabinets matching the décor I approved of perfectly. I head over there, heating water for the French press then adding the ground coffee. When it's ready, I pour the hot, black liquid into my mug, carrying it into the living room.

I've done it for ages, it's a routine I developed akin to many others. Order helps compartmentalize my deviant desires, keeps me fixed on being a decent human. Organization means I know I'll have my fix of being a voyeur behind my computer screen even at times like these when shit hits the fan.

It compels me to remember I'll always remember I have this other routine, that breaking it will end very badly for everyone involved.

I pace toward the window to overlook the neighborhood that's come to life this morning, what the sounds I heard in my room look like. I'm fully prepared to absorb the fall colors under the early rays of the sunshine pushing past the clouds, to enjoy the first apartment that's totally and completely mine.

I'll Be Watching You

However, my plans are short-lived. The sight in front of me freezes me in place. The neighbor's drapes have been left rolled up, and now in daylight, it's giving me a view into a really fucking familiar setting.

The striped shaggy rug, the gray couches. The precise auburn shade of the hardwood floors and the low, gray wood coffee table in the center of the living room.

This isn't some stranger occupying a space several feet from me. Not a man or a woman whose opinions of my body don't matter to me.

This apartment belongs to *her*. I jerked off to her legs when they wandered around it aimlessly. I came many times to the innocuous video of her black-painted toes on the delicate, arched feet as they tapped on the coffee table. Fisted my cock as I watched her stroke her bare torso on one of those couches.

I just know it. It's hers.

Still, to make sure, I step forward, given the living room is empty.

Yes, this is her place. These are her pieces of furniture.

No.

The false denial is fleeting.

There's no denying it. No running from it.

It's hers.

Eva Marks

My heart pounds. Blood and adrenaline barrel through my veins, pulsing behind my ears. The noise blocks out that of the city beneath me, the rush blinding me from seeing anything other than the apartment of the woman I don't only come to, but actually, in a sick way, have grown so attached to.

She's no longer protected by a network of IPs, nor is she shielded from the sick side of my personality.

A decision is made at that moment; I'll have to move out, to prevent any invasion of her privacy in the future, accidental or…not.

"Hi," the woman in Seraphine's living room mouths while waving her hand shyly.

I've been too preoccupied with saving her, with becoming her real-life silent defender, that I haven't noticed her approaching the window.

Her appearance surprises me and soothes me in tandem. My self-loathing and the need to put a distance between us wilts, becoming a distant memory.

On any other day, I'd say she impacts me more than any other human. Just by using her voice, just by showing parts of her body doing absolutely nothing or talking about her day or how she wants to be tied down, she thaws the icy parts of my soul.

This morning, seeing her live, her impact reaches far deeper. Her face, her pure angelic almond-shaped eyes, and burgundy-colored hair

I'll Be Watching You

draping in eaves down her slim shoulders, the entirety of her serves as a blow to my stomach.

Though there's more to it than her physical beauty. Something in me screams that even if this woman had a third eye, pointed elf ears, or a green-colored, Shrek-like ogre face, my feelings toward her wouldn't change.

She's just…Seraphine.

When her brow furrows, I snap out of my delirious state. Looking unhinged, staring at space, will only scare her, and despite needing her far away from me, I don't want to scare her.

At least I hope she isn't, that Seraphine isn't standing there because I raised her hackles by glaring into her apartment. She doesn't deserve to be subjected to me. Nor do I deserve her compassion for crossing a line.

I raise my hand, fingers splayed, rigid, waving her back.

I'm cool. I'm calm.

Most importantly, I am not a voyeur.

"Hi," I say, grateful for sounding like myself even though she can't hear me behind closed windows.

A part of me, the part that cherishes her, needs our interaction to end there. She hinted to me that I crossed a line, and I got the message loud and clear. We'll both move on.

But since observing and deducting sums up what I've done for the past twenty-something years, I know better.

She's not deterred. She's not repulsed. She doesn't want me back in my lane.

Seraphine walks closer to her paned window, unlocks the latch at the center, and shoves the bottom part up.

Standing there in a tight white cropped T-shirt like she described in one of her podcasts, her navel ring glinting in the sun, I know this woman wants to talk.

She really shouldn't.

Turning my back on her would cement me being a creep, and so choosing the lesser of two evils, I stay.

I mimic her friendly action, approaching the window to lift it. The cool breeze sweeps in, but it hardly touches me. I'm too aware of her.

"Hey, neighbor," she greets me as soon as the final barrier between us is gone.

Her voice rings truer in real life, raised and confident to be overheard over the city's life beneath us, yet soft and warm. It's addictive. It makes me crave things, sick things like bottling it up, savoring it for whenever I desire. Or worse. Keeping *her* in a bottle. For life.

"Morning." My lips twitch in reaction to her. A semblance of a natural smile, a gesture almost no

I'll Be Watching You

other person gets to see on my face. I explain myself, "Sorry if I overstepped, I just moved in and I guess I'm still a little lost on where and how to look."

"Don't worry about it." Her grin widens. Again, not worried. Too innocent, too trusting. Too open for her own fucking good. "I mean, yes, the woman before you barely acknowledged me, but I don't mind it if you do."

Yeah, she definitely caught me. She's being gracious about it and about permitting me to do it again. Still, I understand what violating privacy is. I'm the definition of it.

"I apologize nonetheless."

My eyes seal onto hers. Despite myself, I memorize every line and curve of her face, trying to gauge what her eyes are saying in the distance. And they really speak; they say she's not repulsed or bored by me. Moreover, they slide down to my bare chest.

Another mistake on her behalf.

The longer we watch each other, the more the voyeur in me tries to pry its way out of the strict cage I've had him locked in.

I almost succumb to the primitive urge festering inside me. To this need.

I crave to slip a hand below my boxer briefs, whip out the heavy bulge between my legs and come while her unsuspecting eyes only see my arm jerk up and down is ever-powerful.

Lucky for Seraphine, my obsession and adoration for her silence those voices in my head.

I hold firm in place. I'm not that person who will violate her without her consent. Not now, not ever.

I'm an exemplary neighbor. Yup. That's what I am.

"Apology not accepted." It feels like something shifts in her too. The innocence remains, then topped with a side of daring. Teasing, even.

"We're practically roommates,"—she bites the side of her lip, twirling a lock of hair around her finger—"so really, by all means, you're welcome to…watch."

An open invitation.

Her consent.

It's all I needed. I'm going to accept it.

No. No way. I'm fucked in the head to even consider saying yes. A free pass to be a part of her life would fuel the fire that's already simmering and brewing inside me. There's no telling if and when I'll be able to contain it after that.

If I'll be able to stop myself from watching her even on moments I know she wouldn't want me to. In the moments she'll crave her privacy the most, that's when I'll be there, by my window, hovering in the dark and watching her.

Which is exactly why I need to say no. I won't do it to her.

I'll Be Watching You

When she rubs her forearms, I latch on to the opportunity it provides to relieve her of my presence. To save her. "You should close the window before you catch something."

"Okay." The playfulness on her features dims.

Hurting her pinches at my chest. I curse myself inwardly for being this cold to her. For the confused frown that mars the sunshine that's been there a second ago.

It's the right thing to do, I repeat in my head. *The faster she's out of your reach, the better.*

"Enjoy the rest of your weekend." I grip the casing of the window, about to snap it shut.

"Wait!" she calls over the street's noise.

Not a cell in me can refuse her. I stop, quirking an eyebrow.

"You didn't tell me your name."

Shit.

Giving her my name isn't what's making my molars grind against one another. It's finding out her real one.

After today, after this moment, there will be no turning back. I'll have what I've longed for and hate myself for having it. A piece of the most intimate information about her.

Nothing will change on her side. I'll still be her neighbor.

For me, on the other hand, there will never be letting go of her once I have her real name.

But here we are. My opportunity to crawl back to the shadows is as viable as jumping out the window and landing on the pavement unscathed.

Impossible.

"Emmanuel Calvert."

"Hi, Emmanuel."

My name on her lips gets my dick so hard I have to stifle a groan. One of my older fantasies clouds my vision, and I wonder what it'd sound like if I had my face buried in her pussy and my fingers deep in her ass.

When I save her from whatever hurdles life throws in her direction and become a man who's capable of dominating her world instead of being an undeserving onlooker.

I'm doomed. I'm fucking doomed.

I have to find it in me to release her.

"I'm Sloane," she says louder to overcome the sound of a bike speeding in the alley separating us. "Sloane Ashby."

"Sloane." The name rolls on my tongue like a fine, aged whiskey. Smooth and fiery and has me craving more. I tighten my hold on the window, pushing it halfway down. "Nice to meet you. Enjoy the rest of your weekend."

"You too." She bends to where the window isn't closed. "See you around."

I nod once, hoping for her sake she won't.

CHAPTER FOUR
Sloane

Breakfast for dinner. That's what I'm in the mood for this evening.

Feels kind of fitting a day after my calm and organized world has been flipped over on its head.

One minute I'm in my room, editing the truly superb stalker fantasy I recorded the other day, the other I'm stunned even harder by talking to my new neighbor. My God, even his name is impressive.

"Emmanuel. Beautiful name for a beautiful man," I whisper to the three eggs I have left in the fridge. I remember everything about yesterday, remember him, which is also why my drapes are rolled up today.

Yesterday when he looked into my apartment unabashedly, there wasn't a single part of me that didn't tingle from his inspection.

I'm used to having an audience from all over the world, have been during the four years I've run my little podcast and vlog.

But as I found out from the moment my new neighbor came in, I still have some issues in that department.

Because while my viewers can't see my face, while I remain anonymous to them, this is not the case with Emmanuel.

He's more than just a random observer. He's the man I came for on my recording chair, the handsome stranger who made me *feel*.

He's my neighbor and it's more intimate, sure, but it's also *him*.

And he had his eyes on me. He's perusing my living room with something else than a casual curiosity about what was on the other side. His look was thorough, studying, almost penetrating. It was so deep it was visible from all the way to his apartment behind two glass windows.

Then I got greedy, became jealous of my own freaking upholstery and rug and coffee table. I longed for these blues to be fixated on me. An insistent, relentless craving dragged me to the window to demand it, too.

Any timidness I might've had blew out the window at the face of my resolve—quite literally since the winds started singing their autumn tune—

I'll Be Watching You

and I decided to finally, finally, ask for what I wanted.

He might've been in a relationship, might've told me to mind my own business. A man like him who wears the air of authority like a second skin would've had it in him to blow me off, easy.

But he didn't. His cold attitude turned out to be everything I'd dreamt him to be, on top of his handsome exterior and that fine thin layer of light hair on his chest leading to a happy trail below his low-hanging sweats.

He possessed this kind of inner strength that exudes everywhere around him like a sphere without having to show it off by spending hours at the gym or raising his voice to a high obnoxious volume.

He's the kind of man my insides melt for, his somber expression and rugged voice the building blocks of my fantasies. The guy to bend me to his desires, claim me as his, see into my soul. Through his commands, I knew he'd drive pleasure and desire wrapped in a sheath of dominant care to my existence.

A burning scent filters in the air, infiltrating my daydreams about my neighbor.

"Oh, well." I twist my nose as I fan the now almost brown scrambled eggs on the pan with a dish towel. "Was definitely worth ruining for this sweet memory of Emm—"

Eva Marks

The words catch in my throat, my tongue heavy and incapable of finishing the sentence. A thick coat of electricity engulfs me from head to toe, sending a prickling sensation all over my skin.

I'm not alone.

I don't have to cast my gaze up, though, to gauge the intruder's identity.

I already know.

And yet, I do it. To see *him*. I lift my eyes off the scorched dinner-breakfast, up to the newly occupied apartment across my window.

In the darkness of the early evening, two beacons of light stare back at me from a lit-up living room. Two blue headlights pointed straight in my direction, attached to a face wearing a sealed expression.

Emmanuel Calvert stands in his apartment wearing blue trousers and a gray buttoned-up shirt. He's in the center of his living room, not as close to his window as he'd been yesterday, but he's there.

Looking.

He has to know he's as visible to me as I am to him, and he doesn't shy away from it. There isn't an ounce of apology in his observing gaze like there was yesterday.

Shameless, stoic, partly interested in me, Sloane, partly analyzing me like a butterfly under a microscope.

Watching me.

I'll Be Watching You

My neighbor gets a good look too. I left all the lights on here for that exact reason.

The warmth in my stomach and swell between my thighs demand I act through the haze of lust.

It takes me a moment to find my bearings and design a plan. Coming off too strong won't bode well with him. Yesterday is all the proof I need. He seems so astute that I assume something simple and mundane like starting a conversation or asking him if he wants to come over will end up in his boredom and refusal.

But staying stagnant is off the table. The fire inside me grows and curdles my blood, calling me to do something. My arousal soaks through my panties the more minutes tick by of him studying me, my nipples tightening, becoming sensitive and achy, poking through the thin fabric of my tank top, minus my bra.

Which I forewent on purpose. My sheer dusty-pink tank top clings to my skin, leaving nothing to the imagination.

Yes! I'll start there.

I drop my spatula to the stove on top of what should've-been-scrambled-eggs, venturing around the counter where he can see all of me.

My gaze remains steady while I hope his will drop to my chest. He doesn't, although to my delight he does move. Something about me must awaken something in my neighbor because he takes a step and a half forward.

As I lean back on the counter, one of Emmanuel's arms crosses his torso while he rests the opposite elbow in his palm and pinches his chin.

I remain still, though I long to rush forward and open the window.

If I walk forward, stand somewhere between the couches and the window, the bottom part of my body will be blocked by the apartment's walls, and that's a big no-no. Granting him a view of me is intoxicating, and my heart drools at Emmanuel's solemn attention.

My mouth almost drools too.

The overwhelming desire for him and the need to prolong our wordless encounter turn me ten times more brazen. I reach up to the strap of my tank top, spinning it between my fingers.

He takes a step toward me.

I pull it down my shoulder, feeling it taunt the skin on my arm like I'd love for my neighbor to do. My right breast is about to spill out.

I'm doing it.

I'm about to flash someone who knows my real name, my face, where I live. Not a stranger.

Someone I want to be intimate with. Someone I wish would take me out to dinner and be this incredibly self-assured man to tell me he supports my career and thinks it makes me awesome instead

I'll Be Watching You

calling me names like an attention-seeking wannabe actress.

It must be him.

I'm ready for it.

Except…

Emmanuel spins on his heel, and in a confident, decisive stride switches off the light in his living room.

Then he's gone.

I gawk at the empty space in front of me, not sure what to think of it.

I couldn't have been wrong about him.

He was there. He stared.

There's no way I imagined any of it.

And maybe that's the worst of it. That he stood, had his fill, and ended up not liking what he saw.

Maybe I was too quick to believe in coincidences and knights in shining armor when they were not there.

Maybe he thinks less of me like the others had.

A wave of embarrassment washes the heightened temperature of my body. The heat leaves me in an instant, my pulse slows, and each thud of my heart pains the cage guarding it.

With a deflated sigh, I go about cleaning my kitchen; my hunger is all but gone. I walk around the apartment, not caring that my lights are on, and my body is exposed to someone who doesn't care.

Eva Marks

Because this evening taught me a valuable lesson. My new neighbor might tick many of the boxes on my perfect partner list, but me? The only box I tick on his list is that of disinterest.

CHAPTER FIVE
Emmanuel

"Emmanuel, could you come over and take a look at the results on this one?" Arnie, the senior scientist who works in one of the teams I manage, asks me on my speakerphone while documenting some shit on my computer that any other scientist could've done.

"Give me a couple of minutes," I grunt back at the enthusiastic team leader who works beneath me.

Usually, my replies to these types of calls consist of *yes*, or *be right there*, no matter what documentation, emails, or protocols need to be answered. Our research and advancements here at GeneOrg—our white lab coats notwithstanding—bring out the color in my life.

I believe in the cause we're working toward. One of these days, hopefully in the near future, Alzheimer's, Parkinson's, MS, and many conditions others will be reversible thanks to companies like ours. If I can change one life, help one person, then I'll die a happy man.

My heart might be damaged and closed off to the idea of loving and maintaining a romantic relationship—not counting my obsession with Seraphine-Sloane. Doesn't mean I'm a heartless, uncaring man.

Imagining shedding a sliver of light on the darkness in the world is the force driving me to push my teams harder, and I find immense joy whenever we reach the smallest milestone.

That's my every day. Today, though, my mind refuses to play along. The effects of last night are a relentless beast sinking its teeth into its prey, relishing in drawing blood. Seeing Seraphine slash Sloane give herself to me so freely, it did that to me.

I wanted to take what she offered. I was seconds from gripping onto it before she had a chance to retract her salacious suggestion of stripping.

Her innocence, her kindness. She led me into believing staying there to watch isn't a violation of any kind, isn't predatorial.

If I waited for another second for her supple breasts to be released from her top, I have no doubt she would've been okay with me pulling my cock out of my pants. I think she might've even expected me to curl my fingers around my shaft, stroke it until I came to her distant image.

She had, after all, invited me to do it.

I'll Be Watching You

An invitation I couldn't accept.

I couldn't fucking do it. She would've been trapped in my web of deceit. It'd still have been a violation.

In the past, I'd obsessed about her in the space where she permitted it. Had touched the screen to imagine I was stroking her navel ring or falling asleep with her sweet voice in my ears.

She, on the other hand, has no idea who I am. Couldn't possibly picture her plain, unremarkable neighbor as a man who keeps his dark desires of lurking on women locked down.

As much as I ached for her, as much as I craved to have the real-life Seraphine stripping for me while I got off on her naked body and devotion to me, I couldn't. I protected her by refusing to let myself indulge in this immediate pleasure.

It pained me in ways I hadn't known to disappoint her, leave her hanging like this. If not for the devotion I held for her—the woman who up until last week had been admired, yet an unknown—I would've stayed.

I would've shown her just what I did in my bedroom behind the slammed door a second later.

My cock turned so red from my fist fucking it, she would've been able to see it from her apartment. My lips parted when I chanted her name to the emptiness in my room following my orgasm that seemed to last for an eternity.

And yet she didn't, because I forbade it. By turning away from her, I put an end to this.

I'm a proud, cocky man. I know my worth, I know I'm smart. I know what I know and what I don't. *Love* isn't one of those things, but what I have for Sloane feels like the closest thing to affection if I believe what the media is selling.

So, I did what I had to. Otherwise, not only would I have violated her, I would've snapped. The line in the sand the computer had drawn for us would've dissolved into nothing, ending in the expansion of my obsession.

By now—given I would've agreed to what Sloane suggested—I might've done something reckless because of it. Like, show up at her door.

Fixation, adoration, love, obsession, whatever noun I attach to it, would've flared, would've come to life.

All I need is one push in that direction.

That's how much I want her. That's how much I need to stay the fuck away.

Except denying her hasn't made the need go away. I'm not supposed to be hard behind my desk, shouldn't be rude to the people who work under me when they've done nothing to deserve it.

"You don't have to," Arnie continues, his speech less confident than before. "It's not the breakthrough we were looking for, just a small step forward. If you're tied up with paperwork…"

I'll Be Watching You

I roll my tongue across my teeth to hold back a curse. Arnie and I have worked together for the past five years. He's been loyal to the company, to the cause, to me. He, of all people, doesn't deserve this.

He's not the target of my current frustration.

I am.

"No, no." My voice sounds an inch less like that of an asshole. It helps that my dick isn't hard anymore. "Nothing more important."

After hanging up, I fix my coat, push back the chair, and get the hell out of my office. I punch in the secret code to the lab assigned to Arnie and his team, press my thumbprint into the scanner to get inside.

It's an impressive lab. All of our labs are. State of the art. The funding and profits of GeneOrg afforded the company one of the most impressive labs in the field. We asked and were given top-of-the-line equipment, brand-new computers, and orthopedic chairs.

Each room is built to accommodate three round workstations, desks, and lockers while maintaining enough space between them to allow us to move freely.

I nod toward the small groups in the various workstations closer to the door as I approach the last one.

"Hi," I greet Arnie and Denver, the student who does her internship at GeneOrg.

They're hunched over their microscopes, neither straightening when they hear my voice.

My senior scientist with his black hair pointed in every direction holds up a finger for me to wait. He's not being rude; he's in the middle of testing.

"Three, two, one," he whispers before his lab timer beeps and vibrates from where it's clipped on his chest. Only then he stands to his full height, grinning at me, then at Denver. "Yes, it's demonstrating the same behavior again. How did yours react?"

"Same." She hops in place, clapping her hands excitedly. "Could it be…does it mean we can move forward to the other tests?"

"We'll have to document it before that." His intelligent, black eyes dart at me. "And before that even happens, I'd like the boss to have a look."

Denver swallows, suddenly realizing I'm there. The redheaded twenty-year-old spins to face me, slow like a child checking for the monster under her bed. Her cheeks match the coppery color of her hair, and her lips pinch into a tight line that conveys her nervousness.

My stern, no-nonsense attitude brings out that type of reaction in people, especially new ones. Another reason to keep Sloane at an arm's length. Her podcast might skirt on the dark side sometimes, but after catching the sunshine in her yesterday, I get

I'll Be Watching You

she won't want the shadow that I am to obscure her radiance.

"Oh, r-right, of course. Hi, Professor Calvert."

"Miss Denver." I nod once, my usual response curt and to the point. "Hello."

"I—I'm sorry. Let me just..." She rushes to remove the microscope slide she examined, her feet shuffling to get out of my way. Then she clings to a lifeline of what must be my cold stare on Arnie's shoulder. "Here, Professor Calvert. The station is ready for you to observe."

There's an uncomfortable twinge in my chest at her skittish behavior. Sloane doesn't deserve this behavior, yes, though young Denver doesn't either. I appreciate my team members. I ask for a lot from them, and the ones who stay deliver results that should earn them my encouragement every once in a while.

Except nothing in my past taught me how to act around women other than being strict and guarding my heart.

I have to remember she's done nothing to offend me, that I'm not attracted to her or interested in a relationship with anyone other than...

No. I can't want that. I won't even entertain the idea.

This isn't the time either. I'm here to work.

"You've done nothing wrong."

Eva Marks

It's an attempt to appease her. As the head of my department, I aim to be respected, not feared, to encourage enthusiasm in the people under my command. But my tone is still stern, and once again, when she flinches, I realize I've failed.

Yeah, I'm not the man for Sloane, nor will I ever be.

Keeping that in mind, I revert to the one aspect of my life in which I'm never a disappointment. My work. I lean over the microscope Denver prepped for me, waiting for Arnie to slip into the tray a new slide.

I unlatch my compact lab timer from my coat and glance at Arnie. "Time?"

"Thirty seconds." His chest puffs with pride at our success as a team. "Reaction time is thirty great, goddamn seconds."

My apartment is dark. Other than the lamplight near the door, all the lights are off.

Just how I left it.

Just how I'd prefer it to be for the rest of the evening.

If Sloane would see me… If she tries something again…

I'll Be Watching You

The ache in my groin tells me exactly what I'd do, how I'd accept her taunting and take what's offered.

I need a fucking drink to stop thinking of her nipples that perked when a gust of cold wind grazed them, to demolish the repeated sound of her saying *Hi, Emmanuel* from my head.

For two years, unbeknownst to her, this woman owned me. She had me pretending I was her defender. The lover who, by her side, wouldn't be afraid to be himself—or even better, the man she'd adore and, in turn, he would find it in him to touch her.

To own her.

Now, when we're separated by a meager shout of *hello*, I've become a different kind of savior. I'm on my knees rather than on a white horse, knowing all she'd need to do is ask and I'd run to the better world she has in store for me.

For us.

The streetlights of New York and the dim glow from the lamp are enough for me to maneuver around the apartment. Before I move toward my whiskey near the window, I glance up, examining Sloane's living room.

Dark, too. Not a single light is on. Not a lamp, a phone, or a television screen gleaming somewhere inside. She could be out with friends, or the early sunset had her nodding off.

Either way, the chances she's up, sitting, or lying there idly with the lights off are slim to none.

She's not there. I can walk freely, grab my whiskey, head back to the kitchen, pour myself a glass, and off to bed.

A weird, reprimanding thought rises in me. I face the board of GeneOrg every quarter. I go against a process that's happening in the human brain every day when I come to work, against nature.

I shouldn't be intimidated by a woman or fear my own loss of control.

No. The answer is no. I'm not afraid. I'm cautious of this precious gem.

Tomorrow, when a day will have passed, I'll switch on the lights. Look at her, and find it within me to walk away if she decides she still wants to strip for me.

Today, however, the shadows are my friends.

I hang my bag, shrug off my tan jacket, and traverse the living room to where my whiskey awaits. My fingers curl around the neck of the bottle. I'm ready to retreat to my bedroom to start my night.

A light comes on across from me.

"Fuck," I hiss.

Blood rushes to my groin, my heart beating like a motherfucker on a racetrack. Without so much as turning my head to cast my eyes up, I'm already hard.

I'll Be Watching You

And famished. So very famished.

She waves.

The basic knowledge I've been harboring since this morning lingers. She presents me with an opportunity. I'm launching myself at it.

Both of us might live to regret it, but there's no stopping this train.

Carefully, I twist in the direction of her apartment. In the seconds I moved in for my drink, she switched on the lamp on the coffee table I recognize. The light glows around her, enabling me to see her clearly.

She's an explosion of fire, her waves of burgundy hair running wild down her shoulders. A few of the locks graze her collarbone, and the rest are at her back. Her chocolatey eyes are wild as she tries to talk to me through them.

My gaze skims lower, down to her breasts. She wears another skin-tight tank top, gray today, and she doesn't hide the fact she doesn't have a bra on. Or that she's cold now that her window is open.

I part my lips slightly, picturing how I would suck on one of those nipples, soak the fabric until Sloane is a whimpering mess under my command.

But that's not happening. Not her, not with a guy like me.

Another wave.

Returning to her face, I notice the subtle smile playing on her lips.

Fucking wonderful. Instead of removing myself from the situation, I made it worse. She's amused. Interested.

In me.

I fasten my grip on the bottle, my body halfway in the direction of the inside of my home. I have to control this.

Then a large piece of paper appears. Sloane's holding it from both ends, and it has seven digits written on it in black marker. A phone number.

I blink twice to make sure I'm seeing it right.

I am.

It says *CALL ME*.

CHAPTER SIX
Sloane

I smile, praying my expression doesn't betray the hesitance in my heart. And if it does, please don't let him get the wrong impression and think *he's* the thing I'm not sure about.

Well, he sorta is, but not in a way that I don't know whether I want him or not. I do. What causes the slight tremble in my heart is the fear he might not want me, to get a second no to cement his rejection.

My eyes widen watching him do the exact opposite of what he did yesterday. He rolls up his sleeves, revealing those lean forearms.

It takes a whole lot of willpower for me to keep from leaning forward, from gravitating toward him. I summon every ounce of my inner strength to stay in place.

Eva Marks

I made the first move. It's his turn now. On his terms. I don't move a muscle, don't even blink while I gauge for more of his reaction. For the response, I'm crossing my toes.

His blue gaze pierces me through the distance separating us, studying me in return. He analyzes my sign, maybe wondering what I want from him, why I wrote it. Maybe considering just how weird this woman asking him to call her is.

He's contemplating, considering it.

Though there's still no cell phone in sight.

Nothing but his intense glare.

With nothing left to do, I give Emmanuel time.

A notion kept nagging at me throughout the entire day, something telling me Emmanuel didn't blow me off last night because he wasn't into me. He was. The way his attention lingered on me until the moment he left, I'm confident he definitely was.

This morning, I stopped my self-pity to think about what exactly went down between Emmanuel and me. Knowing *my people*, the men and women who view my channel, and the stuff I read about voyeurs and people who have trouble communicating and forming relationships helped me reach this conclusion.

How Emmanuel had his face stuck into my apartment, I could assume he had a little bit, if not a lot of that, in him. He wasn't put off by me. He

I'll Be Watching You

looked at me. He held my gaze and burned me a million degrees hotter. It happened.

And so even though he ought to be a functioning man—his suit and apartment are the proof he works—for voyeurs, communicating with the women they want is either tricky or it isn't their thing.

His appearance, the waves of strength flowing from him, they fueled my need and my incessant wondering of him. I had to have another shot at seducing him, at testing where Emmanuel stood.

If it was a matter of timidness, I was more than willing to abolish it.

Even the strongest men cracked in some places. They were human. As was Emmanuel.

But I couldn't push him hard for it, which is why I called off the cookies for now.

The sign, the invitation, and the space for him to decide—those are what I assumed would form the best solution.

I'm a buzzing ball of energy, listening to the noise of the street below me and the pounding of my heart. My clit flutters with every second of his intense inspection of me, my mind reeling with expectation.

A thousand livewires connect inside me all at once when I finally see him pulling his phone out of his pants pocket. His expression is the exact stoic one

I witnessed yesterday, and yet it doesn't matter. He's calling.

Me.

"Hi, neighbor." I drop the homemade sign, allowing him the view I saw his eyes were drawn to earlier—my breasts. "You're home late. How are you?"

He doesn't speak for a full, excruciating minute, observing me through his indecipherable glare. I don't mind. Today we dance to the rhythm he dictates.

"Will you please close the window?" He sounds irritated. "You'll catch a cold."

He cares. I pull my lips together to suppress a smile and do as he asked.

"Done."

"Sloane, there's something I have to tell you, before…" Emmanuel trails off, pinches the bridge of his nose, then talks again. "I know who you are."

"I kind of shared it with you yesterday," I start, my inviting smile returning in my attempt to communicate that our familiarity is okay through two panes of glass. "And you introduced yourself back, so yeah. We both know each other now."

"No. It's not what you think."

His shadowy figure becomes clearer with the single step he takes toward the window. The ice-cold I've seen in his eyes seeps into his tone, but there's something so hot about it too.

I'll Be Watching You

It's hard to decipher when there are these barriers between us. I'm itching to go against what he ordered me to, pull up the window to gauge his expression better.

Emmanuel's next word and the longing attached to it freeze me in my place. "Seraphine."

The lungs I thought were functioning a minute ago give up on me in one quick second. Not air comes in or out of them. Not even a gasp.

My compassion and affinity toward my viewers do not equal wanting them to know my home address. Plenty of them wouldn't get here even if I sent an Uber to pick them up, not like I'd ever take that chance.

I hired a computer expert to keep my location secret through a network of IPs to ping across the world on a complex web for those who'd consider taking the fantasy a step too far.

And now…now one of them didn't simply find me.

He lives across from me.

"Sloane, please." His voice is direct, a command that soothes instead of frightens.

My wheezing slows, the hand massaging my chest bringing me comfort. However, this isn't where I should be. I should be on my laptop, searching for a new place, preferably on the other side of the state.

I hear LA is nice. Sunny, palm trees, beaches.

Anywhere but here.

I have to hide.

"I need to go. I appreciate your honesty. Truly."

The blurred edges to my vision dissipate the more my escape plan forms into a real thing. The power in Emmanuel's stance drives serenity into mine, so my voice is calmer, but I'm still very much a woman on the run.

"Sloane, stay." He calls for obedience, though nothing is degrading about the way he says it, like he might be talking to a pet.

He also refers to me by my real name, rather than calling me Seraphine, and that realization gives me a serious pause. While his eyes assess me and demand—what, I'm not sure of—I consider the meaning behind the name he chose to call me.

A predator, a man obsessed with my online persona, wouldn't have said, "Sloane." A man who couldn't see any further than Seraphine and the arousal and lusts she inspires in him wouldn't have cared for the real woman who portrays her.

He wouldn't have revealed his secret. He would've used me, lied to me. Would've played along because it's pretty fucking obvious it wouldn't have taken him more than a *Go on* for him to get me to strip and do his bidding.

"I need to explain. After that, you're free to hang up in my face. You're free to run, and I swear I

I'll Be Watching You

won't chase you or offer anyone any information about you. You have my word."

The cool air surrounding him drags me further from the erratic state I'm in and into safety. It might be a false one, but I'm powerless against feeling it nonetheless.

"Do I have your permission?"

Heat seeps through my body. A kindling fire that starts in my lower belly and drifts lower and hotter, each licking flame obliterating my anxiety. Without realizing it, Emmanuel reveals himself as the man I imagined him to be—dominating yet kind, just the right amount of rough to not scare me, but make me feel protected.

It'll be wrong of me to refuse him the chance to at least tell me his side.

"Okay." My feet carry me to the wall. My nipples caress the glass of the window, and the prickling cold of the outside strains them until they're hard points. "I'm listening."

The blue, fathomless oceans of Emmanuel's gaze drift down my chest for a second. He growls, scowls as he looks up, then inches forward.

"First thing you should be aware of,"— his attention on my face feels as though it costs him to keep it there—"I'm a voyeur. I know who you are, so it's only fair that I'll be level with you about who *I* am. I'm not a bad man. I don't beat off to women without their consent, don't plant hidden cameras in women's restrooms or changing rooms. Truth is…"

Cut open and vulnerable, Emmanuel doesn't cower from me or his confession. He's stoic in his place. From where I stand, he's more of a ruthless warrior than a man confessing to a quality of himself he's clearly not proud of.

Because the way he delivers his message has nothing pathetic about it. He owns it, at least in front of me, and he treats it as only an honorable person would.

And that reveals a lot about his character, rather than his circumstances.

The sound of a long intake of breath matches his parted, masculine lips. "Truth is, Sloane, I haven't been watching anyone but you for the past two years. You feed my obsession. Only you."

It's my turn to suck in air. I'm not frightened anymore, no. Trepidation isn't why I'm utterly speechless and plastering one hand to the window in a dire attempt to balance myself.

What unsettles my heart, causes it to palpitate like a manic bird trapped in a cage, is how all the stars align in one magical moment. Emmanuel's knowledge of my profession, his acceptance of it, his adoration of me.

He doesn't think I'm unworthy.

Liberty was right. We're still practically strangers, but it's a better starting point than any of

I'll Be Watching You

the past dates I've had for the last four years. It's something to work with, a sliver of hope I'm trying on.

I like how it fits.

"You have?" I whisper. "I am?"

"Yes to both." He nods once, completely in control of his confession.

"Which brings me to my second point." Emmanuel's shoulders rise an inch, his lean frame as intense as a bodybuilder's. "My…devotion, it isn't purely sexual. So given the information you have, you can tell me to close the drapes facing your apartment. You won't have to run either. I'll find a new place. I won't stalk you, harass you, or watch you without your permission. The word of a stranger might not mean much, but that of a professor who works at GeneOrg, whose number and address you have, who gives you the keys to his life to ruin if he goes back on his word… I hope it's enough to make you feel safe."

"No." I press my hand to the window, flexing my fingers on the glass where my warmth creates condensation. "No."

"No?" He tilts his head to the side. Though there's doubt in the single word, he moves forward until he's an inch away from the window.

"No, I don't want you to move out." My voice is breathless. Airless. Drowning with need. "And no, I don't want you to want me any less."

"What do you *want*, Sloane?" A grave quality permeates his voice.

"To be Sloane instead of Seraphine for tonight." I back up to offer him a better view of me hiking my tank top up to reveal my navel ring. "To be your personal exhibitionist, to be the conduit you use for your pleasure, Professor Emmanuel Calvert."

He grunts, shaking his head subtly. At the same time, however, his right hand disappears lower. "You don't even know me. You shouldn't."

"Oh, we will get acquainted." My arousal and attraction speak for me in a sultry whisper. "I will bring you cookies and we will have a clothes-on discussion. After tonight. After you move back until I see you pleasuring your cock, after you tell me exactly who and what you'd like me to be for you. I won't have it any other way."

"Are you sure about that?"

"Do I sound hesitant?"

"You always seemed sweet. You sound it. I bet you even smell it. And that's how I want to treat you, sweetly," he says as if the word tastes bitter in his mouth. "Problem is, tonight, there'll be nothing sweet about what I'm going to do to you."

CHAPTER SEVEN
Sloane

"**I** can take it." I steel myself, piece by piece transforming into his fantasy. "I want to take it."

"Ground rules first." His darkness curls around his voice, pouring into the phone. The shift is so fast, and yet makes so much sense. It's so *him*. "Unless you say *daffodil*, I won't stop telling you what to do once I start, and you won't disobey me."

He's providing me with a safeword. *My* safeword. Several months ago, I recorded one of my podcasts recounting a make-believe experience of me and an imaginary Dominant, one whose face and body I couldn't quite put into detail, but I knew and loved his soul to pieces.

It was everything that Emmanuel appears to be.

Somewhere in the distance, on the other line, I hear the clink of a belt buckle. The soft metal sound, the foretelling sign of this practically stranger about to remove his clothes, doesn't bother me. It thrills me to have him want me and demand it instead of hiding.

I want to submit to him. Fully, completely, unconditionally. There's something about him that stirs a hunger in me, and I trust him. As fucked up as it sounds, I trust this stranger.

And I'm all in. "I won't need it."

"Remember it anyway. Now, open the window." Emmanuel retracts his earlier demand to protect me from the cold, his words ripe with desire. "Let me have a better view of you."

I saunter forward, embedding sensuality even in a simple movement like unlocking the window by slanting my hips and pressing my chest forward. Every gesture is calculated, done slowly, sexual rather than practical.

"You sound like the big bad wolf," I say in a hoarse voice. My Seraphine's voice.

"You have no idea."

"If it means I'll get eaten…" Seraphine takes a little more over me. If she makes him more comfortable, paves the path for him to come to me, I don't see the harm in playing along. "Then I'm dying to find out."

His window is already opened when mine slides up, his hand at what must be his cock, his arm jerking up and down in thoughtful, meticulous movements. Hypnotic.

I'll Be Watching You

So mesmerizing that I'm caught off guard the next minute. "Sloane, leave Seraphine out of this. Let me have you."

A whimper rushes past my lips, my eyes falling on the world between us. I'm frozen, trapped between joy and disappointment. Between being flattered by his desire to be with the real me, and disheartened for worrying whether I've been wrong about him, whether he too will ask me to quit my job.

"Look at me." The sharp deliverance of these words jolts me, giving me no choice but to comply.

"I love Seraphine," he confesses, filling my insecurities with flowers. "She's a gift you are exceptionally talented at delivering. You should always have her in your life. Always."

"But?" Despite the distance, I search his gaze, hoping to find out if he's being honest. If he won't take that back once he comes.

"But *you're* here, now." His arm resumes the motions it stopped. Emmanuel walks backward until his pants are in my view. His open fly.

His dick in his masculine palm.

"*You* make this cock hard." He strokes it once, twice, allowing me a show of his own. Even from feet apart, his thickness is visible. And mouthwatering. "I'm like this for *you*, I want to get to know *you*. And when I fuck my hand tonight while barking orders and telling you whether you can come or not, you *will* be Sloane for me. Do we understand each other?"

I swallow around the dryness of my throat. What I wouldn't give to be where he is, drop to my knees, to have him own me. But it's his game to run, so I bottle up my request, being aroused by the simple act of obedience.

My lips part as I grunt out a, "Yes, Sir," my own hand drifting lower.

"No, no, no." Turning into a statue, he shakes his handsome face. "You will obey me with your body, not just your words, or this all ends."

I let the hand lingering at the top of my waistband fall to the side. And then I realize something, a truth I'm insanely confident about.

Emmanuel is not a Sir. He's not detached, demanding Master I dreamed of bowing to and serving. There's something about him... Not tenderness. Nothing gentle. Nothing visible at least.

It's some kind of an invisible aura, telling me he'll be cold but that he'll also make me love every second of it.

For that, he's not entirely a Sir. He's more of a, "Sorry. Yes, Daddy."

His chin bows, blue irises lifting to haunt me. "Good girl, Sloane."

"Thank you." Shivers rake my body, excitement prickling my skin. "What else would please you?"

"Got wireless earbuds, baby?"

I'll Be Watching You

I hum at the husky change of his voice at the word *baby*. "Yes, Daddy."

"Go get them. I'll put mine on too." He taps his screen, then mine vibrates with a message from him. A link. "Play this on your speakers in the background while you do."

He claimed he had no sweet plans for me tonight, he showed me not a shred of a delicate man beneath his shell, yet his insistence to set the mood means I haven't misjudged the caring qualities in him.

The attraction I have for him multiplies at the gesture, and I'm powerless to do anything but stare and nod.

With his cock out proud, a man completely unabashed once he slips into his character, he turns around to head back to the hallway. Only when he's gone do I sprint into action.

In my room, I pull up his playlist on my laptop and connect it to the speakers in the living room. There's a comfort in him knowing the ins and outs of it, removing the need to explain, the sense of awkward beginnings. None of that with us.

And even though he has leverage when it comes to my personal life, I realize the first song on his playlist doesn't surprise me either. "Way Down We Go" by KALEO could easily be the soundtrack to the darkness Emmanuel radiates, the sensuality of it increasing the craving in my soul.

"Emmanuel?" I whisper, still out of his sight, shielded by the drapes in my bedroom.

I'm unsure whether I'm allowed to speak or not, but I'm incapable of remaining silent.

"Bring the nipple clamps you have there, then come out to the living room. Quick." He ignores the hesitancy in my question. "Don't make me wait."

It amazes me how a man who gets off only behind a screen manifests this dominant role so well. Better than any book I've read about the topic, and just as confident and exerting his control as the Doms who allowed me to observe them in a sex club I visited.

I hadn't had the guts to be a part of their scenes, never felt it was quite right despite the heat that bloomed in me from watching. I wanted to be dominated, to be someone's tool for pleasure and derive pleasure from it in return. But it was never *it*.

Never the exact right person or moment.

Never until Emmanuel appeared in the apartment across from me, until he made everything so perfectly right that I don't need to doubt anything.

The autumn breeze lashes stronger into the living room. It stings harder that I've come back from the warmth of my bedroom. I don't dare put my arms around me, don't consider rushing back to change into a long pair of wool sweats.

I'll Be Watching You

I'm Emmanuel's pawn. A willing one. Because I trust him.

And when his intense gaze meets mine again, I know the trust is warranted because he heats me more than ten radiators ever could.

"There you are."

In the time I've been away, my neighbor has lit up two lamps inside his living room. He's no longer a shadowy figure with two blue gems glaring at me. He's this slim yet rock-solid man I talked to yesterday, and he's smirking at me.

The tilt of his lips appears warm and cunning in tandem. His clever gaze raises questions that have nothing to do with sex in me: What kind of professor is he, and what does he like to do in his spare time other than watch me?

Who is Emmanuel?

I'm getting ahead of myself. I'm fully aware of who I am, except, what can I do when he just has that vibe that captures my soul and involuntarily makes me wish?

Nothing. The answer is nothing but roll with it.

"Here I am."

"Drag a stool into the living room and switch on the lights. I need to see you. All of you." His hand moves while he speaks, pinching the head of his cock, sliding back down, then up again.

Since the delicious treat of seeing him come depends on my compliance, I waste no time obeying.

"Good girl." He lets out a satisfied growl. "Sit on it, lean on the back, and spread your legs to either side for me."

I do as he says, sliding onto the stool, placing my feet on the footrest, and placing the nipple clamps on my belly. The crotch of my tight boy shorts and panties rub against my swollen clit, and I bite down on my bottom lip to stifle my own pleasure at the friction.

"What was that?" Emmanuel presses a finger to his earbud. "I thought I heard something."

Through the window, where I'm perched on my stool, I'm not one hundred percent sure my blush is visible to him. At least, I haven't been sure, not until he smirks.

"Spread your legs wider."

My breathing begins to match his, heavy and laden with layers of lust. I answer, "Yes," though my body doesn't get the memo.

"Open, Sloane." His warning gets me to react. "Beautiful. Tease your little cunt and let me listen to what my commands do to you."

The strokes of his cock are unhurried, and so is his voice. He's smooth and seductive, direct and irrefutable all at once. "Now, yank down your top, show me your tits, pinch them as you grind against your shorts."

I moan before he even finishes his sentence, immobile from the immense sense of need.

"Do it for me, Sloane. This fucking instant."

"Daddy." I stare at him dead in the eye, grabbing the top of my tank top and drawing it as low as it will go above my belly button.

"Release it."

And I do. The cotton fabric hikes up to catch on the underside of my breasts. My roaming mind imagines that the wind licking at my needy skin is Emmanuel's tongue and lips.

"Are your nipples hard?"

"Yes." I pinch them, hoping he at least sees the outline.

"Fasten the clamps on them," he says, grunting at the sound of my pained groan when I do. "Just like that. Put two fingers from each hand in your mouth, get them nice and wet."

He waits for me to have my lips stretching to continue, his tight voice matching the dark stare a few dozen feet can't hide. "Take them out and stroke the tops of those beautiful mounds like it's my tongue doing it to you."

The satisfaction stemming from my compliance echoes in the room. I wouldn't be surprised if it reaches Emmanuel's apartment or even the entire building.

Eva Marks

I've been taking care of myself, of my sexual needs, for so long. So many months of being the only person touching myself. Emmanuel's presence over the phone eradicates this loneliness. Having me follow his lead emulates the sensation of a lover caressing me, here with me.

He's torture and magic. Flame and ice. Everything.

"That's a good girl."

I open my pinched-shut eyes to find him perched on his table, studying me intently. His praise reverberates through my body; his glacial gaze anchors itself in my soul.

"Thank you, Daddy." I'm meek and rubbery, needing him here yet knowing not to ask for what he can't give.

The spit has almost dried out, but I still pleasure my nipples, not stopping until he says so. I glare at him deeper, the bottom of my feet digging into the wooden support to hold myself upright.

"That pretty pussy of yours,"—I accept the compliment since I'm certain he's had his fill of Seraphine's more intimate videos, and I love that he has—"I want to see it. Move the stool to the window, take off your shorts, and give Daddy a view of your cunt."

In my most crass podcasts or vlogs, I'm nothing compared to Emmanuel. The ecstasy coiling in my stomach sears me from the inside, pushing me almost

I'll Be Watching You

over the edge. I'm afraid, but it's not Emmanuel who sparks the sensation inside of me.

His words and his deliverance of them terrify me. Another one of them and I'll come instantly, wailing and gasping for the man who has yet to lay a finger on me, praying to someone up there that he will.

Listening to his erotic groans propels me to move forward, to do as he bids. I won't ruin this fantasy, won't do anything he doesn't demand, including orgasming without his permission.

I hop off the stool, shoving my shorts and panties down and away. Living on the top floor, I'm thankful for the knowledge we won't have viewers, though it is possible I would've acted just the same even if I had an audience.

I'm that desperate, that longing, that much yearning to please Emmanuel. I follow his orders, striding to the window with the chair behind me, then slide up, opening myself to him.

I do it as Sloane would do. Less seductive, less sensual, and yet one hundred percent myself. It brings me relief so profoundly, and I don't know how it's possible, but I'm more wet than before, dripping.

"Beautiful." He's analytically scanning my body while leisurely stroking himself, making me long to be used by him all the more. "Such a beautiful fuckdoll taking my instructions so well."

Eva Marks

His voice carries from my earbuds to the rest of me, a waterfall draping down my neck and nibbling on the sensitive spot where my shoulder starts. I shiver. "Yes. Thank you, yes."

"Will you be able to take my cock that well, little Sloane?" Beyond the turmoil in my heart and the lust clouding my eyes, I notice a hint of a smirk that tilts his lips to the side. "While I fuck you the whole night and break you again when you're sore the morning after?"

"I will." My moan reverberates through the phone while I part the swollen lips of my pussy for him to see. "I want you, Emmanuel. You and your big cock inside me. At night, in the morning, bend me over on your lunch break. I want you."

"Like I said, you have no idea what you're asking for," he growls, but despite the threat, he doesn't stop fucking his hand.

"Yes, I do."

Since he doesn't deliver any other order after that, and I'm on the verge of being suffocated by the all-consuming agony to have him, I improvise. Just a little.

His attention flicks between my face and my gaping pussy. That is, until I mimic what I'd imagine he'd do if he were with me, sliding my middle finger into my cunt, raising it slowly to play with my clit.

I'll Be Watching You

The blue of his eyes becomes fully immersed to the apex between my thighs, his hunger as vivid as the hushed curse words he's spewing.

Then he says, "Stop it."

Like a complacent doll, I do.

"You're being a greedy, disobedient little slut, Sloane." The words are free of malice, yet their power is ever strong, pummeling into my chest where my attraction to Emmanuel develops and grows. "Your little hole too. Now you'll have to be punished. Slap it."

My jaw slacks. This part has never played into my fantasies. Maybe because I haven't considered it before. Maybe because…

"Did I stutter?" He stands from the table, his lean frame taking up the entire room somehow. "Slap. Your. Pussy. Twice now, that you disobeyed me."

Granting him my last piece of free will—other than the option to safeword—I lift my palm from where it touches my clit, and smack it. The first contact is dull, but the pain that turns into pleasure still comes.

I'm moaning when I land the second strike, harder this time, heightening the sensation of the sting and the high I got before.

"That's more like it."

The speed of Emmanuel's jerking grows faster. My tongue swipes my bottom lip with the desire to have his cock on it, to taste the precum that must be dripping on his fingers.

"Rub yourself where it feels good, spread those juices, and make that cunt glisten as if I'm there eating you out."

The back of the stool digs into the soft of my back as I writhe uncontrollably, pushed slightly due to the force of his stark command and filthy words. I straighten myself a second before I slide out.

"Careful, baby." His command remains fierce, looking out for me past his need to come.

"Yes, Daddy." I bow my chin to my chest, then do as I'm told.

An easy task is given how dripping wet I am. My index and middle finger circle every part of me, slick and slippery.

"You're a good girl, aren't you?"

"Yes," I pant, or he pants. The both of us are a breathing, heaving mess and it's beautiful. "For you, I am."

"You want to come with your Daddy?"

"Please." My moan is inelegant but it's all I have in this purgatory of teetering so close to the edge without crossing it. "Yes, please."

"Two fingers inside and pinch and twist your clit. Only when I tell you, do you pull it hard and then release it." His grunt reaches right into my heart. "I'll hear it if it doesn't hurt, so you better do it right."

I'll Be Watching You

I don't really know Emmanuel. The trust I have in him stems solely from his confession and a basic instinct telling me I can. The torture on my clit sounds painful, but I do it anyway, confident in his care for me.

"Oh, my fucking fuck," I growl through clenched teeth.

"Look at me, Sloane." His voice is equally strained. "Those pretty eyes should be set on me when you come. It's my orgasm. *Mine*."

I'm out of my mind; endorphins and clouds and the heavens above swirl in my head as I curl my fingers into the sensitive spot inside me, as I torment my tight, aching nub.

"Say it." He huffs in my ear, "Say it's mine, and I'll let you come."

"It's yours," I gasp the words I've been wanting to utter to the fictional men in my dreams, the men who are nothing compared to what Emmanuel is. "My orgasm is yours."

"Do it. Pull out the clamps with one hand and pull and release your clit with the other."

A fierce, life-altering climax wreaks havoc inside of me. Before my sanity is lost for what feels like forever, I heed his command. Blood rushes south and north in one insane hurricane attack, elongating and heightening what already hurts so good.

And I scream.

Emmanuel's visceral growl follows, his strokes slowing, his breaths leveling out. His eyes hold mine captive while he wipes himself and tucks his cock inside his pants.

"Such a good girl." The sudden tenderness in him contrasts with the harsh man he was two seconds ago, though it doesn't give me a whiplash. It's natural, soothing, carrying me down slowly to the earth. "You're more wonderful than I've ever dreamt you to be."

"Thank you." The tingling in my heart is only partly due to my orgasm. The rest belongs to the thrill stemming from making Emmanuel proud.

He approaches the window with slow and careful movements. I adjust my tank top back in place and slip on my panties and shorts, then do the same, until he and I each lean our forearms on the windowsill.

Wind whips at my face, scattering my hair around me. It's colder the more I return to planet earth, a weakness I hide by staying stoic, refusing to let this evening end.

"Why don't you come over?" he asks, and for the first time, I notice a slight dread or a tremble in his smooth voice. "Or I can come over to you, fix you something to eat, hug you… Talk."

He's offering the final step in a scene, aftercare. I would've leaped on the opportunity too, had it not been for the hesitancy in his question. I realize

I'll Be Watching You

exposing himself has been a huge, monumental step as is. Last thing I want is to push him. I don't want him to be overwhelmed and run off on me.

"Tomorrow, maybe?"

"All right." His face contorts briefly one minute, returning to his stoic mask the next. "Please close the window, though. Make yourself a tea, have something to eat. A hot bath, even. Think you can do it for me?"

I hope my lopsided smile says what I'm trying so hard to hold back. Affection, gratitude. "Yes, Daddy."

"You're something else." He exhales quietly, his eyes gazing down while his lips tip up. "Night, Sloane."

"Night," I say so low it's almost a breath, disconnecting the call despite craving him worse than a drug.

Then I pull down the window, turn my back to him, and say to the empty room, "Until tomorrow."

CHAPTER EIGHT
Emmanuel

I said it. I fucking offered her what I couldn't bring myself to offer to a single soul in the entire universe.

Shared intimacy.

Not sex. That hurdle I got over in college. A couple of my lab partners were available. I was available. I was a replacement for them, and they helped me not be a virgin. A fair exchange.

That was until one day I thought it could be more. I asked one of them out. She had a cute smile and it made me believe even a boring, unimpressive man like me had a chance.

I didn't. She was already over to the next guy, the one she was *really* into.

After that, I haven't had any other attempts at conforming to society's standards. Dating hasn't been in the cards for me.

Then came Sloane.

I'll Be Watching You

This gorgeous gift who looked at me through my window, she had every reason to run, yet she didn't. She called me Daddy. Promised to drop by later.

But as the day went by, I realized how all of it must seem from her end, and how she probably wouldn't be here. Words spoken behind a sex haze and a rush of endorphins couldn't be trusted.

It's not that I think she's a liar. She had pain lacing through her, a fierce pleasure after which there was no one to administer aftercare to settle her back to reality.

I got off on plenty of BDSM porn before I stumbled upon Sloane's podcast, usually veering off from professionals and opting for ones by private individuals. Watching them helped me realize the importance of each step, how high the bottoms were. It couldn't be helped.

So, if she wouldn't knock on my door today, if she regrets what she said or what we did, I wouldn't hold it against her.

And yet I can't get her out of my head.

The incessant preoccupation with Sloane doesn't let go as I leave the subway. It doesn't remove its clutches as I hike up the stairs, taking two at a time to exit the street.

I'm overtaken by it, so much so that I don't bother rolling down the drapes when I get home incase she didn't mean what she said.

Matter of fact, I don't look anywhere other than the floor, trying not to think, to go against my nature. My brain functions like a problem-solving machine. For issue X, there's always a solution Y hiding somewhere. For science problems, managerial matters, all of it, I've been consistently a clear, level-headed solver.

Romantic stuff, though? Sifting through a woman's feelings? That's when the world isn't black and white anymore, when I admit any solution I might have will be the wrong one.

I'm powerless, helpless against the ethereal enigma that is Sloane Ashby.

And yet, contrary to my logic, my heart refuses to admit defeat. A fire in me burns so brightly that my blood rustles and crackles beneath my skin. I'm desperate to see Sloane. To conquer the deviant hunger in me to orgasm just by looking at her. To do *more*.

Even if she doesn't want to. I'm able to control plenty of things in my life—my career, the order in my apartment, not touching myself at the sight of women who didn't ask for it.

This, this *stalking* of Sloane, this breaking the promise I made to her, it can't be helped.

I steal a glance in her apartment's direction, noticing she's not there. She will be, though, and soon. It's only a matter of time, given it's her workplace.

I'll Be Watching You

Everything in my place here needs to be darkened by then. I turn off the single light in the living room, go and change into a black T-shirt and matching jeans, grab a chair and position it in the space where the living room turns into the hallway.

Anticipating her.

I'm patient, sitting in my hiding place. Nothing's more important than *her*. While I'm there, my memories run back to her mass of burgundy hair, her trusting eyes, her eagerness to please me.

She comforts me, whispering in my ear that what we shared last night was not a figment of my imagination.

Seconds turn into minutes. Confirming my theory, not many of them pass before she saunters into the living room. A smirk tugs at my lips, watching her prance from the hall into the space I know so well, the space that belonged to us yesterday.

Her building, much like mine, must have a boiler system to warm the apartments because once again she's wearing those ass-baring cutoffs she had on before and a bright orange tank top that covers very little of her skin.

There's a low, thudding ache pulsing inside me. A longing for my songbird's voice. I could call her. I could ask for her to tell me something, anything. But sitting here, observing her is just as satisfying, or at least that's what I tell myself.

Eva Marks

Blood rushes to my cock, my erection growing in my jeans during the time I follow her movements around the house. It's becoming harder to breathe when her butt cheeks taunt me on her walk to her kitchen, when her breasts spill over as she leans on her kitchen island. Or—and this one's probably the worst—is her pout.

Since I'm seated at the edge of my apartment and she's on the farthest side of hers, the details, curves, and shape of her body shouldn't be this visible to me.

Thing is, they're etched into my memory now. Like she is.

Yeah. Exactly like I thought.

After yesterday, there's no fucking way I'm ever letting Sloane go.

CHAPTER NINE
Sloane

Someone's watching me.

And I'm not talking about my subscribers.

My gut clenches, lead coating it with the assurance that there are eyes on me this very minute. I'm alone in the house, yet I don't feel it.

I haven't given anyone permission to violate my privacy. None of my cameras are on, my mics are turned off, and my bedroom door is locked.

I ought to be scared.

I ought to be terrified.

I ought to experience some sort of terror.

But the one sentiment coursing through me as I cross to the kitchen for the umpteenth attempt today at the perfect cookies isn't trepidation.

It's excitement. The thrill of being under Emmanuel's watchful gaze sends a chill down my spine, one I do my best to conceal. Though he's not visible from where I stand—and won't be, with the lights on here and his off there—I sense his presence.

The smallest acknowledgment will ruin this game. For him and me alike.

I'm not toying with his heart. This is how I turn my lemon of a situation into lemonade.

I promised him I'd come over today, and I've been craving it ever since. But I promised Emmanuel before we even talked that I'd make him cookies, not a moment sooner.

Which is what I've been trying to do, all day long, nearly twelve hours. And by trying, I mean failing. Not a single batter was good enough, causing me to throw away each cookie I tasted.

On my third trip to the grocery store, April the clerk raised a skeptical eyebrow in my direction. After that, I simply ended up buying supplies for cookies to last to the end of a decade and called Liberty.

"I have one just for you. It runs in my family since my grandma's grandma used to bake it for her husband," she said about the cookies about an hour ago. "It has to work. It always does."

"Awesome, then I'll bake them real fast." I began rummaging through the grocery bags, placing the products in Liberty's recipe on the counter. "Then shower while it's in the oven, and go over to him."

"Not so fast."

I'll Be Watching You

"Huh?" I pressed my phone between my ear and shoulder.

"The only glitch to it is that you have to let it chill in the fridge for a whole day before anyone can eat it." I could hear the smile in her voice because it's a known fact that best friends love torturing each other. "I forbid you from tasting it and throwing it away either. It won't be perfect until tomorrow."

And so, reluctantly, I accepted her rules and I'm giving it a chance.

I hated this fucking waiting to my guts. But what choice did I have? I needed this to be perfect, couldn't accept doing a half-assed job to satisfy him. Not in bed and not cookie-wise.

But yeah, waiting sucked. My impatience got the better of me while I'd been lying in bed, reading a book Liberty recommended—a smutty romance that didn't help.

At all.

Because with every word I read, my mind was bombarded either by the memory of Emmanuel's voice, his charged glare, or the ease with which he handled me. Like he was aware of his sheer force, could guess how it would affect me to a T.

Beep, beep, beep, the timer on my phone went to have me go turn off my old oven. My desperation grew, knowing I'd have to wait another twenty-four hours, and then it happened.

His glare made itself known.

Eva Marks

The consistent heat pulse thrumming between my thighs intensifies as I walk around the kitchen, each exhale I breathe coming out as a gasp.

Another whole day without him?

Hell, no.

Well, maybe not in the traditional sense.

From here, from where I stand, I have to be enough, I tell myself.

I'll speak to him in his love language for the time being, allow him to lurk in the shadows and watch me.

I bend down, shut down the oven, and open the door.

Do not *take the cookies out an hour after they're ready*, Liberty's voice echoes in a warning in my head, so I leave them there.

It's a good thing these cookies are spoiled, too. This way, Emmanuel won't see them, and my surprise won't be ruined. I straighten myself after switching the oven off, heading back to my room.

There, I undress, taking off my tank top, underwear, and short jeans, changing into my lace white robe, the only garment on me when I return to the living room.

The sense of being under Emmanuel's gaze intensifies, his ice-cold nature blending with the warmth his attention lashes onto me. It takes insurmountable strength to stay in my role and not relieve my aching nipples or rub myself down there.

I'll Be Watching You

When I do, it'll have to be timed. Perfected for him.

It'll be a clear message that I'm his. I gave him ownership of my orgasms yesterday. Today, I'll let him have the rest of me. Almost.

With my eyes glued to the floor, I head straight to my window, opening it. Today has been remarkably cold, the unforgiving wind billowing around me, messing my hair.

Though it doesn't really matter. I'm not the onlooker here. My eyes shouldn't see, shouldn't look for the man I'm seducing.

My robe—similarly to my hair and according to plan—is subjected to the wind's force and opens up to expose my body. I exhale slowly, reveling in the chill of the evening flicking on my breasts and pussy.

I stand there, my hands pressed to the ledge, grinding my crotch between them. And then I feel him a second time, stronger and more powerful than before in the kitchen.

It's Emmanuel. I feel him at his place, how hot he is for me. I know it's him, deep down to my bones.

He's not touching himself, either. He's noble. In more ways than one. He did say he won't abuse our living arrangement unless I give him permission.

Thing is, I want him to.

Next time we'll meet, I'll give him explicit permission to masturbate to me whether I'm aware of it or not.

In the meanwhile, I keep giving him a show, playing my part.

I'm the performer acting for my favorite viewer, and I'm about to put on a show of a lifetime.

I throw my robe to the side, completely exposed. Emmanuel's hot attention makes my blood boil, my clit swell, tightening my nipples into sensitive little buds.

Remembering his voice and commands, I pinch one and relieve it, then move on to the other. Instead of my fingers, I picture it's his teeth biting down, clamping on me, even drawing blood.

My lips part when I say his name without voicing it.

Something in me knows without a shred of a doubt that Emmanuel's erection presses hard against the pants he's wearing. That his jaw clenches, that his nails dig into the inside of his palm in his attempts to keep his promise, even though I failed to deliver mine and go over to him.

Behind the drapes of my eyelids, I see his blue ones. They're intense and hungry, wanting me and me alone. I see his hands that stroked his cock turn on me, grabbing my jaw and cupping my pussy, his thumb running in circles around my wet nub that belongs solely to him.

I'll Be Watching You

I recreate his touch, grinding my hips round and round on the ledge. The friction from the concrete and metal has my muscles clenching.

So close, I'm so, so close.

But since I'm not allowed to finish on my own, I do the one thing that has to be close enough. I beg, repeating the word *please* as I feel myself tighten, about to snap from the immense need that consumes me.

Do it, I hear his voice in my head. *You're a greedy whore, but I'll allow you this one.*

I might be making things up, although it doesn't feel like it. It doesn't feel like it at all.

And with his silent permission, I come to the open window, orgasm for his eyes alone, sucking in gulps of air while another piece of me becomes intrinsically *his*.

CHAPTER TEN
Emmanuel

Morning came and went.

I haven't called Sloane the day after the private show she put up for me, nor has she given any sign of life.

My inner turmoil grows as the nerve endings in my brain attempt to solve the unsolvable.

Her.

Maybe I got her signals mixed up. Missed the "no" in her "yes."

Maybe there was an underlying intention in *I'll come by later*, meaning I'm only useful to satisfy her exhibitionist needs and nothing else?

Maybe.

No. The electricity that crossed between us twice already, that transcended the limits of physical touch and bonded us together, no fucking way it

I'll Be Watching You

was one-sided. She didn't imagine me agreeing to her plea to come. She felt it.

After a long day at the lab, I'm finally home and alone with my thoughts, pacing into my bedroom and back.

Crack, crack, crack, my shoes go.

In that repetitive, incessant noise, a decision is made. I'm going to get her.

I'm going to go big or go home, literally. Just walk over to her place.

It'll be miles out of my comfort zone or my sexual preferences—except this, this isn't sexual.

I don't need my dick to be hard to be a Dominant. The possessiveness I feel for her, the obsession to have her in my arms, it doesn't revolve around my orgasms or hers.

I want her, and I'll have her.

I storm outside my bedroom, out to the hallway. Grabbing my keys is the last thing I do before pulling open the door and in five minutes, I'll be knocking on hers.

A shriek reverberates from my doorstep to my ears, added to the noise of a plate clattering on the floor at our feet.

Sloane's and my feet.

It takes a minute to realize it's her. I see her there, I recognize her adorable nose, soulful eyes, and waves of brown-reddish hair framing her face like the sun, and gradually it sinks in.

"Hi." Her breathless greeting finalizes it for me. She's here. And standing close to me at that.

Her scent is just as I thought it'd be, fresh and clean with a hint of sweetness. She smells like the ocean, of the wild. She fixes her eyes to mine, the caramel in hers swirling into something dark. Another side of her I'm falling for. Another that gets me hard.

Another aspect of her personality that has me wanting her so fucking badly.

My self-doubt or concerns about rejection all fly out the window. Tossed aside, crashing on the pavement in the alley that separates my apartment and this beautiful woman's home.

The desire for intimacy—not just with anyone, with her—trumps them one by one. It climbs on top of them, crushing them under its heavy weight as it rises to the top of my consciousness.

I'm no longer Professor Calvert, nor am I the onlooker who lurks in the shadows.

Her presence transforms me into a one-track-minded animal. The repeated message coursing through my head is clear as it is demanding, telling me to take her. Possess her. Own her.

I inch forward until her soft areas graze my hard ones.

"Hey, Emmanu—"

It's impossible for me to let her finish her sentence, to allow those lips another word without

I'll Be Watching You

pressing mine to them. I wrap one arm around her back, and my other hand cups her nape to tilt her head up and claim her lips.

"Sloane," I groan at the pliancy of them, at the ease with which she parts them for me.

While still kissing her, I drag her inside the apartment. I untangle my hand from her for a single second to slam the door shut behind us.

Something crashes behind me, but fuck if I care. Fuck if I give a goddamn shit about anything except her, her tongue, her teeth, the texture of her lips as she molds them into mine.

"You." The entire weight of my body slams her into the wall to the left of the door.

"Me," she pants.

When I can't stand her lustful gaze, can't take watching the darkness in it calling to take what I haven't even thought I wanted, I grab both her shoulders. I spin her to the wall, manhandling her to push her face to the side and press myself against her.

"You're here." My hands lower to her waist, my nose trailing the length of her neck up to her ear. "Why?"

"I—" Sloane gasps as my fingers slip between her and the wall and cup her pussy above her black pair of yoga pants.

There's no helping the deep-seated craving that's been rooted in my soul for her. I'm feral in my desire, so much so it pushes my affinities to the side.

She'd let me watch if I asked, but I don't want her to.

"Oh." The long sound of her moan drones out my insecurities and fuels my fire.

Keeping pleasure for her, keeping my cock away from her, these thoughts don't cross my mind for a second.

But it'll have to be built up in steps, which is why I hold her where she is, the way she is. I'll make her moan and come; I'll ask her why she changed her mind. I can get answers as to why she's here.

All with her back to me.

Her eyes begin to spin toward me. I flatten my palm on her cheek, forcing her back to the wall. Sloane's puffs of air dampen my skin, short and quick like she rasped during our phone call two days ago.

I'm harder than I was a second ago, a feral man bathing in his desire.

A sliver of lucidity prevents me from attacking her further, not before I know she's really into it. Two nights ago, she said she wanted my dark side. She wasn't lying, but we had a safe distance separating us.

I can't figure her out, not yet. I need answers. "Why are you here?"

"Cookies." Her arm glides up on my wall until it's perpendicular to the floor and pointing at the door handle. "I baked cookies," she says through her

I'll Be Watching You

mashed profile, a hint of a smile hiking her lips to the side.

The memory of shit clattering and breaking around us returns to me. It tears a crack through the cloud of lust, mistrust, past the not-love-but-more-like-obsession I have for her.

That's the sweet fragrance playing with her hair. Chocolate, vanilla, and sugar.

She baked cookies.

This isn't just about sex, be it dark or vanilla. Maybe. I can't assume.

"You want me to fuck you?" I bite down on the soft tissues at the crook of her neck, grinding myself onto the soft crease between her butt cheeks.

"Yes—no." She arches her back, however little I let her.

"Which is it, little songbird?" My middle finger dips into her folds, separating her through her pants and pushing the fabric into her hole where I rub the slick entrance.

"Emmanuel, I can't think." She speaks into my palm, her tender lips brushing against me with every word.

"You saw this nice neighbor," I continue, squeezing her front and driving into her back. "Your admirer. Maybe you're lonely. Maybe all you need is a good screw—"

"No!" Her fierce denial gets me to stop. Sloane's body remains still beneath me while her eyes peer into the space my fingers make for her. "I'll be lying if I said I don't want it, that I could concentrate on anything but your dick driving into me over and over again."

Her ability to deliver such dirty talk does little to surprise me. After all, I know her. Except now she says them to *me*. I freeze, waiting for what else she has to say.

"Fuck." Sloane sighs, she lifts her hand to cover mine, and plants a kiss on the inside of my palm. "It's too fucking early to say it, but the last two days, I *felt* something. I came here to do what we talked about. To get to know each other."

Through squinted eyes, she assesses my silence. It's not until she begins to wriggle in an attempt to free herself from me that I grasp how wrong I've been.

How deeply I offended her.

Determined not to let her go, I push her back into the wall.

"I got it all wrong, didn't I?" She tries to get away again. I don't let her, molding myself into Sloane's body and pressing my mouth to her neck. "I should leave."

I remove my hand from her cunt, whirl her to face me, and bind both her wrists above her head, then lower myself to level our gazes. The inner predator hiding in the depths of my soul comes out to play, and it's after her.

I'll Be Watching You

"Does this feel like you've got anything wrong?" I growl before our mouths crush together a second time.

The way they connect, mesh and pry the other one's open is different from our first kiss. Gone is the element of surprise. The profound emotion I'm trying to bury peeks through without my permission. Thing is, I stop caring. There are no more misunderstandings, there's only Sloane.

"Does this"—I don't release the pressure on one of her wrists while I shove her other hand to my painful hard-on above my pants—"give you the impression that I'm not into you?"

"Don't…don't lie. You don't have to be nice." Seeing her earlier confidence simmer eats at my insides. I'm pulling and pushing her like a doll, and she still doesn't believe me. "I misunderstood yesterday. I'm sorry. I'll just… Just let me go. I'll leave."

"Songbird, the one thing you're misunderstanding…" In swift, fluid movements, I yank down the zipper of her hoodie, throw the garment to the side. I continue by removing her long-sleeved black shirt, twisting it tight like I'm about to wring water out of it, "…is what I was trying to tell you last night and again a minute ago."

"What?"

"You talk too much." I pull her head away from the wall, wrapping the shirt around her face. "It's time you listened. Be my good girl and bite."

CHAPTER ELEVEN
Emmanuel

"That's it." I pat her head, stroke her locks, cradling the side of her neck while applying the slightest pressure on it. "Since I own your voice for tonight, if at any point you're uncomfortable, tap twice with your hand, understood?"

She nods, glaring at me from below. Fear has nothing to do with her wide eyes, though. She's in awe.

So am I. It's an unfamiliar emotion I keep locked behind a safe in the very back of my soul, but Sloane sets it free.

"Let me tell you a few things." I take one step back, admiring how docile and receptive she is. "For two years I jacked off thinking about you."

Sloane's nipples poke from under her silk-and-lace black bra. I push down the cups to expose her, making her more vulnerable and attentive as I pinch the erect peaks and twist them between my fingers.

Sloane whimpers behind the homemade mouth gag when I pull them toward me, releasing a strangled cry when I release them all at once.

"Your voice, your body, the scenarios you painted, they turned me into a hungry fucker."

No longer hiding, I permit Sloane to gauge the man she claims she wants for all his sickness. I unbuckle my belt, undo the button of my pants, roll down my fly.

"Any sensible man would be driven crazy by you." My cock is heavy in my palm, freed from my boxer briefs as I fist myself in Sloane's face.

Her eyes trail my movements, run up my body to meet my stare, remaining there. How she holds herself, fierce yet submissive, desperate to catch fire yet accepting the wait for her torch, it's remarkable. And very fucking hot.

"But in reality, you weren't just talking to my dick." I press forward, sliding my hand past the waistband, past her clit, curling two fingers into her pussy. "You didn't exist just to make me want to pound into every hole in your body until you broke for me in my fantasies. You weren't simply getting me to come five times a night on those times I really. Fucking. Craved. You."

She sighs, fluttering her eyelashes and pushing her hips into my touch.

I'll Be Watching You

"Something about you"—I stroke her inner walls to the rhythm I pump my shaft, the heel of my palm attending to her clit, my forehead resting on hers—"something in the cadence of your voice, in your free-of-judgment attitude, it drew me in."

In the silence between us, at the moment when my words sink in, I observe her. Dilated pupils, darkening cheeks, generous thighs that clench and ache for me.

"I've been enchanted, even enamored by you. Obsessed."

It should raise red flags, to realize how nothing I say intimidates her. Quite the opposite, she melts into my touch, grunting and drooling for a man she hardly knows. Though it's not me I'm worried about, it's her. Any other man, any man with less self-control would've hurt her.

My woman.

Doesn't matter now, though. I have her, and I'm never letting go.

I stop rubbing myself, returning to grip her slender neck. My fingers dig harder into her skin, angling her head up so that less than an inch separates our eyes, and only her T-shirt stands between our lips.

"The past three days, though?" I coax another muffled scream from her when I bite her neck and shove a third finger into her arousal-soaked hole.

Eva Marks

I look up to Sloane's sharp eyes as if her body is dire to demand its climax while her heart knows its place, understanding how thoroughly it's mine.

"They've taken it up a whole other notch. I need more from you. So,"—using my pinky finger I collect the dampness seeping to her inner thigh and circle Sloane's pucker—"say the word and I—"

"Yes!" I think I hear her say behind her shirt, an assumption being affirmed by her enthusiastic nod.

Her fingernails rumple the sleeve of my shirt with more desperation the faster I pump into her. I can't stand another minute of being robbed of my songbird's voice, no matter how much pleasure I get from watching her saliva drip down her chin.

Can't take another stretch of a second without burying my tongue in her mouth, not probing her lips wider apart, and having both my palms gripping her jaw and commanding her to be mine.

And she gives it to me; her breathless scream fills the air as soon as I rip off the shirt blocking her mouth.

Her chest undulates beneath me, gasping for air, burned by desire. She tries for my shaft that's grinding to the soft of her belly, but I'm faster, curling my fingers around her wrist.

"I'm clean." Nipping on her knuckles, I lower to the floor, one knee after the other. "You?"

"Yes, on the…oh, oh…" The music of her labored breaths accompanies me, encouraging me

I'll Be Watching You

while rubbing my nose to her clit and wrenching her pants down after getting rid of her shoes. "On the pill too. Christ, fuck, I'm on the pill."

"Good." From my place on the floor, I stare up at the curve of her belly and her breasts, ending my trail on her eyes. "Because once I'm done marking your cunt with my mouth, I'm going to own it with my cock."

I don't hold back to wait for permission or understanding. I pick up Sloane's quivering leg and place it over my shoulder. Her sweet lips open up, her skin glistening with arousal, the swollen nub in the middle puckered and waiting for me.

"Greedy little clit," I say with my mouth on it; my words are spoken as well as felt. "Gonna love eating you out."

"Daddy," Sloane gasps, begging louder, "Please, Daddy, please."

"Good girl," I murmur one last time.

My tongue swirls in circles to taste her folds, flicking in the center where Sloane is aching for me the most. I return my fingers to probe deep inside her, pushing them in without teasing or making the invasion smooth for her.

But it's not enough. I slap her breast with my other hand and suck her clit hard between my teeth. She screams, slamming her hands flat to the wall she's barely leaning on.

Her whole body convulses into a shuddering, hot, and wet vessel under my command. I've never dreamed of taking a woman like this, even in my darkest fantasies.

Then again, it's Sloane. It's *her* clean scent, *her* juices dripping down my chin, and *her* unintelligible sounds that paint my apartment in colors of her surrender and my control.

She makes me become more of myself with every passing second.

"You want to come?" I keep pumping her sopping hole, moving to her other nipple, inflicting torture where my hands, fingers, and soul are. "Want to come on my mouth, have that pussy clench for Daddy?"

The title rolls easily from my lips. Even before she called me that, I longed to take care of her before I met her.

"Yes." Her head thrashes to the left, slightly banging against the wall with her eyes on me. "Please."

"I'm sucking your naughty clit again, little songbird." I scratch what must be Sloane's G-spot because she jerks in my hold. "Count to five, and only then am I allowing you to orgasm."

"Yes." She nods once, her lower lip slack. "I promise. Please. Please, Daddy—"

Her whimpers get caught in her throat and morph into an erotic groan once I'm sucking,

I'll Be Watching You

nipping, and lapping my tongue in all the ways her body responded to earlier.

"One, two," she cries in rapid succession.

"Slower." My fingers clamping and rolling her nipple painfully serve as a warning as much as my voice does.

"Th-three."

I moan in approval, dipping my tongue lower to where my fingers meet her slit.

"Four," she shouts at the change, my tongue then fingers playing with her pussy in intervals. "Five!"

At the last count, my queen clenches around me, gripping me like I'd never want to escape her.

My songbird's sounds of pleasure beat any song the actresses who played Christine Daaé's part in *Phantom of the Opera* ever sang. Sloane's voice rings truer than an innocent's confession given at a polygraph. Explodes louder and brighter than the Fourth of July fireworks.

She creates music so pure, I'm intent on hearing it again. This time, echoing into my mouth.

On my feet, I pluck out the buttons of my shirt with one hand, my eyes not leaving Sloane's for a second.

"You're such a good girl." I stroke her cheek, leaving a streak of her juices on it. "So beautiful, too, wearing your arousal like that."

"That was..." The strength in her voice withers, giving place to nirvana. A momentary one. "That was amazing."

"Turn around." I'm stern and hard, even this naked before her. When she doesn't move, I grab her hips and have her facing the wall. "Lean forward with your hands."

"Emmanuel, did I do something wrong?" Despite her hesitance, she does as she's told.

"If that would've been the case,"—I lean forward, pressing my chest to her back, gather her juices on my cock and slide it along her crack—"trust that your ass would've been spanked raw."

"No, but I thought—"

Running on pure instincts, I slap her ass. Twice.

"Now you've been bad. It's *No, Daddy*, Sloane." I'm massaging and pinching the wounded area to keep reminding her she's mine. "And you'll do well to remember I said I'm going to own you with my cock. We're not done a second before that, or if you say *daffodil*. We clear?"

"Yes, Daddy," she hums like a good girl.

But there's nothing good or kind about how I take her. I shove every inch of my throbbing length inside her cunt in one shove, her walls squeezing around me in response.

"So tight," I growl in her ear.

I'll Be Watching You

My fingers bite into the soft flesh on her waist and ass, my dick pounding into her as hard as she'll take it. And then some.

"Look at this hot little pussy." My voice and her breaths entangle, our gazes never leaving one another's. "Taking all of me, sucking me into that sweet, tight cunt. My cunt."

"It's yours."

"Let me hear you saying I own your cunt, baby."

She doesn't even hesitate. "You own my cunt, Daddy."

"I do, don't I, songbird?" I straighten up, kicking her legs apart and sinking in deeper. "I wish you could see my cock dragging in and out of you. You're dripping on it. Fucking soaking me."

The continuous harsh thrusts, my words—or both—evoke more songs from her lips.

"Wish you could see how I fuck you, how hard you make me."

"I want to."

Slap. "Another day. If you're good."

"Oh, God," she chokes on the short prayer when I pummel into her so hard her body nearly loses balance.

"Emmanuel, Sloane. The name's Emmanuel." An intense orgasm builds inside me, the sense of urgency coiling in my lower stomach. "Say it. Say my"—thrust—"fucking"—a second one, and now my fingers rub her clit relentlessly—"name."

"Emmanuel." My name sung by my angel is everything I'll ever need.

"Come for me." I press one finger to her mound, pounding into her for all I'm worth.

And she does. Her climax tears through her the second mine hits, and I spill my cum into her clenching and unclenching pussy, making good on my promise and marking her as mine.

"Beautiful, baby." Just so I won't miss any part of tainting her as my own, I pull out of her. I squeeze myself one last time, and rub it along the seam of her ass and the start of Sloane's lower back. "Beautiful, and *mine*."

CHAPTER TWELVE
Sloane

The floor plan of Emmanuel's apartment might look like mine, but its interior design couldn't be further from it.

Where I have walls painted in a warm mustard shade, his living room has one brick wall that gives it an industrial appearance, and aside from his couch, the rest is so…white or just dull. Sad.

The walls are white, linens are white, the wall-to-wall closet on one wall is also white. Or some shade of off-white, though in the darkness, at night, they all seem the same. Very, very white. This room's only pop of color is in the bed and nightstand which are made of wood. But it's pine, and yes, very light.

I don't hold it against him or think it's wrong.

When I sit in this pine bed, covered in two white wool blankets, my head leaning on

Emmanuel's chest who hugs me after the shower he gave me. And I'm saddened for him.

Not for him being a voyeur. Especially not for that, otherwise would we even have met each other? Would he have been so accepting of my job?

Some things are meant to be. It's a possibility. But just like he expressed in no uncertain terms that he takes me as I am, that he wants me for me, I wouldn't change his tendencies for the world.

It's because of the colors. Or more likely, the meaning behind the choice of having his home so detached and emotionless. This poor man could really use some love.

For once in a fucking long while, I found a man I care about and who cares back. And to maintain that, I have to and am willing to be blatantly honest. Ready for my soul to be prodded and observed by him much like—and even more so—than give him the control of my body.

I've known this man for three days that feel like a lifetime. That's why I'm sure he won't take it the wrong way.

A man who hugs me as if he's scared I'll crack, who caresses me like being tender to me is his life's mission. A man who soaks in my presence as much as he lets me soak in the comfort he exudes.

We're both naked, sitting against the headboard of his bed. The radiator engulfs us in warmth on top of the building's heating system, but it's nothing

I'll Be Watching You

compared to the caring embrace Emmanuel gives me, the heat of his body, as that offers me a safe descent from the high.

It's then that I feel the safest to delve deeper into who he is.

"Emmanuel?"

"Yeah, baby?" The powerful warrior who seized what he wanted without sparing me an ounce of pleasure talks softly to the top of my head.

In the back of my mind, I begin to wonder whether bringing up the topic is a bad idea. My emotional state could only be described as a serene mess; my thoughts aren't what I'd describe as fully coherent. Whatever I say could come off as judgmental or prying.

I decide to do it regardless while being as gentle as possible.

"Are you sad?"

His low chuckle takes me by surprise. With a tenderness that matches his voice, Emmanuel slides his palms to my cheeks, draws me back to look at me, studying my eyes.

The blue of his is so stark up close that I almost get swallowed in them. They're tender and kind, speaking to me even before he does.

"What makes you ask that?" He strokes my temples with the pads of his thumbs.

"Did you…" I nibble on my bottom lip, considering carefully what I'm about to say next.

"Ask me anything." The side of his lips tilts up. "Here, let me get you comfortable. You'll feel right at home like this."

Home.

My mouth clamps in an attempt to shut down my galloping heart, to not let him see how it affects me. It's a casual thing people say all the time, *My home is your home.* It's nothing really.

I shouldn't read into what's not there. A private man like Emmanuel—it mustn't be easy for him to have me here, let alone let me sleep over or mull this concept of…

Home.

For now, in this space, in the bubble we created, I'm his.

It's more than enough.

Emmanuel arranges us until we're both lying down, positioning my leg on top of his. When I'm still quiet, he trails his fingers along the side of my body, and even though I'm nestled into this heavenly warmth, wherever he touches, goosebumps rise.

"Can I be honest?"

His brow creases, but still, he says, "I'll accept nothing less."

"You only moved in less than a week ago, so I might be getting ahead of myself." He doesn't reply, stop or admonish me. I go on, gliding toward him, flattening one hand on his chest, the other on his

I'll Be Watching You

newly stubbled cheek. "But there aren't any colors around here. And..." I trail off.

"Anything, songbird." He pulls my wrist to his lips and peppers kisses on it. "Ask me anything at all."

"When I peeked at you..."

In seconds that elongate into what feels like forever, the side of Emmanuel's mouth curls into a secretive grin. "*You* were watching *me*?"

"Maybe." I hide behind one closed eyelid. "Yes?"

"When?" The amusement in his smirk and the intensity in his stare clash.

My eyes are drawn to where my fingers graze Emmanuel's bare chest. Anything but those probing blues that'll accuse me of not being truthful with him hasn't granted him the courtesy he had me.

"I saw you when you were talking to the movers," I whisper, but he doesn't let me run from this.

"Hey." He tips my chin up, and I'm doomed, falling hard into the icicles aimed at me. There's no anger registered in them, only pools of a hunter's curiosity. Like he's interested and wants to physically pry the answer out of me all at once. "I've been stalking you for two years. You can tell me if you looked."

"You were honest about it."

I'm too well aware of the importance of privacy. Of consent. Stalking my neighbor then constructing a sexual fantasy around him—that isn't it. Did he listen to that one? Is he connecting the dots, realizing I talked about him?

With an inelegant pout, I try to bow my head again.

"It was bound to happen." Forcing my gaze back up to his, he forces me to stare back into eyes that are now compassionate, a soft gaze I'm not sure I deserve. "Physically, it was impossible not to. We do live across from one another. What intrigues me, though…"

He's going to ask about the podcast. He's going to ask about the podcast.

Fuck my fucking life, I curse inwardly as my cheeks burn in humiliation, *He's going to ask about the podcast.*

"You saw me, and you still wanted to play after that?"

Huh?

"Huh?"

This man and everything about him will cause me to end up in an eternal loop, I'm so dumbstruck by his question. I mean, who wouldn't be?

"I…" His lips pinch into a tight line, his face hardening. He's building a shield around himself faster than I can scream at him to stop. "I never figured I'd be your type. Or anyone's."

And there's my answer. A huge chunk of it, anyway.

I'll Be Watching You

"What does that even mean?" I pry carefully, talking to a wounded tiger instead of a person. "Everyone is someone's type."

"Don't give me that look." The scowl on his face would've startled me into silence had I not sensed that it, too, is a layer in his defense mechanism. "It's a fact. I don't care. My appearance doesn't define me."

"But you're beautiful."

"Don't."

His growl doesn't scare me. His detachment doesn't scare me. Nothing about him scares me.

"Handsome." I curl my fingers around his wrist, guiding it to the wet apex between my thighs. If he won't believe my words, he'll at least have to feel my honesty. "Powerful. Sexy as hell Dominant."

"Quiet," he grunts.

Emmanuel shakes his hand out of my hold, though he doesn't break our contact, flipping to my side and forcing his fingers inside me.

He's doing what I wanted to remind him he's capable of.

Being strong. Being desirable.

Being the only one to claim me.

"I saw your back when the movers were here, that was an accident."

A fuller understanding of Emmanuel dawns on me in a rush. It must arouse him to watch because of how safe it is. It makes my confession easier to pour into the reality we share, free of fear. If he's not *safe*, neither am I.

"The second time was on purpose."

"Shut up." His cock stands erect as steel against my ass, grinding on it, teasing my little hole.

"I won't." I spread my legs for him. "I was curious. And for a good reason. I liked the man on the other side."

"Stop."

Emmanuel's confidence is undeniable. He's strong, sharp, has a very clear idea of the life he's after and, better yet, how he's planning to entwine ours together. To protect me, handle me, and be my soft landing all wrapped up in a neat package.

What he's lacking, what stands between him and true happiness, is believing he isn't an outsider. That he is wanted, craved, and insanely desirable to the point I didn't think I was worthy of him.

"You told me to be honest." I glance back, then have him shove my face into the pillow.

"I did, but there you go, lying to me." He exerts his control over me by leaning on top of me, opening my pussy while burying three of his fingers in my mouth, flat on my tongue. "Coat them with your spit."

I do, choking on him and loving it.

"You liked me being a Dominant over the phone." The heat of his lips on my neck drives me to near oblivion. "Not the image of the man you saw."

I'll Be Watching You

His fingers and my mouth are so wet, dampness trickles down my chin. Emmanuel drags them slowly to the back of my throat, then out.

"That's what you liked. I'm not this miserable person. I like what I like, and that's watching." He steals my breath when he lets go of my pussy, probing his soaked index finger inside my ass. "With you, I want more. So do you, and that's what I'll give you."

"No!" I moan and cry in one desperate call.

"Is that *daffodil*?" Everything stops; my breaths, whimpers, and Emmanuel's movements.

"No," I say truthfully. "What I was trying to tell you is—"

Two slick fingers go past tight tissue and the lit-up nerve endings of my pucker. I'm high on him finger fucking my ass while breathing hard in my ear, flying higher when I hear him spit on his other hand, letting me know he's lubing himself.

"Come here." He leaves my pucker empty only to have it crowded by the thick head of his cock.

"I'll take you, own you, and consume you however I wish. You will be my good little girl"—he presses me toward him by flattening his palm on my pussy, going back and forth in meticulous movements to part me further—"and you will never lie to me."

The *me* leaves his mouth with equal ferocity as the thrust of his hips when he slips the tip of his impressive length into my ass.

"Breathe." His instructions are joined by his fingers stroking my clit.

It's then I remember to do it, noticing how I held air in my lungs up to that moment. Emmanuel is big, really fucking big, and I'm torn and left wanting for more simultaneously. So much so that I forget my words.

"I'll still be here." His lubed length slides all the way in, then somehow feels deeper when I press my head back in ecstasy. "I don't give a shit about being model material if I can be the best man there is for you."

My mind clears at that, like the clouds parting after the rain. Regardless of the pain that slowly morphs into joy by his pummeling in and out of me, I understand.

"I did a podcast about you."

"After our phone call?" He doesn't sound angry. He comes off as self-assured like he really doesn't care whether I think he's handsome or not, and he fucks me like it too. "I'd love to listen to it. Together."

"No." I'm levitating in space, half of my neurons disconnected, temporarily out of order given the amount of pleasure being thrust at them.

"No, what?"

I'll Be Watching You

The other half, meek and feeble yet still there, they tap on my lungs and throat, propelling me to speak.

"Not after. Before." Emmanuel's body is my body, his sweat and mine are one. I'm sure he believes me, and yet he goes rougher, refusing the truth. "You haven't"—I grunt at each penetration—"haven't listened to it apparently, but it's there, Emmanuel. It's there."

His groan emanates lust and relief. His lips kiss my shoulder in reverence, then bite them in angst. He knows this isn't a lie.

"What am I going to do with you?" he says to my skin.

My smile is inevitable, though I rein it in fast. "Whatever you want, Daddy. I'm all yours."

"You are, aren't you, baby?" He slithers his hand up my belly, wrapping it around my throat. He doesn't cut off my air supply, but he certainly constricts it.

"I am." The words I breathe out are barely audible. It's due to the limit he's forcing on me, to the soaring of my heart, and how I'm not grounded in any way, shape, or form.

"Come for me." His palm squeezes and strokes, chokes and releases to tease me. "Let me feel that beautiful throat reverberating with the scream of your orgasm, little songbird."

Eva Marks

I don't hesitate to obey, nor can I hold back the waterfall of my climax from breaking through the weak dam, the last of my resistance.

Emmanuel's name and the symphony of my climax are possessed by their owner as he tightens his grip around my throat by a tiny bit. He elongates the shuddering of my body, then joins me, unloading his hot sperm in my ass.

What feels impossible in the minutes Emmanuel and I are curled into each other becomes an undeniable reality—I love him.

It's too fast. Too dangerous. It might end up ripping my heart out.

Nonetheless, it's the truth.

I have to say it. For myself, sure, but Emmanuel should hear it too.

Saying those three words for the first time isn't something I want to do facing a white wall. I turn around to a man who cradles my face in his palms, who kisses my nose and eyes.

Who speaks to me through the brush of his lips on my skin.

I open my eyes after he pulls back to look at me. "I love you, Emmanuel."

He's quiet for a while, the pad of his thumb drawing circles on my cheek, the heat of his body seeping into mine.

"You really do." His lips eventually crush into mine, eating me alive, thoroughly, deliciously.

I'll Be Watching You

When he pulls back again, he says, "Good fucking thing, because for the longest time, Sloane Ashby, I've been crazy in love with you too."

CHAPTER THIRTEEN
Sloane

"Argh!" I let out a frustrated groan that's been building up inside me for the past hour.

"Why—" I delete the first shitty video of me tapping my toes I made two days ago.

"Does—" Then the three I recorded in the past of me watching the television now are so painfully dull.

"Nothing"—ending with erasing today's shitty winner of a podcast I half mumbled through because it was all crap—"work?!"

My beleaguered sigh might be the best singular sound I've conjured for the past three days.

Ever since the night I fell asleep in Emmanuel's loving arms—who was happy about the cookies but much preferred having me instead, repeatedly—I've been rendered useless to do my job.

The problem hasn't been him. Or more to the point, it has been him, but none of it is his fault. In

I'll Be Watching You

the morning we woke up together, and someone who works with him called. Arnie, I think was his name, told him something turned up overnight and that he had to come quick to the lab.

Emmanuel, who I noticed had been sparse with his smiles, had his lips hiked to one side to match the twinkle in his eyes. I couldn't stay indifferent to that expression, not even when the disappointment of having him leave so soon crawled up and darkened the edges of my vision.

"You understand, songbird, don't you?" He cupped one of my cheeks, eyes tender and intense in equal measures.

Of course, I understood. Whatever happened there at GeneOrg must have been great news for my handsome neighbor and, in the future, for the world population. A little less wonderful for me who, in the span of several days, became greedy for this man's attention.

I acknowledged my whirlwind of emotions was bigger than I thought, larger than my body was able to contain. In the crisp autumn morning to the soundtrack of the wind tapping at his window, I even had the sense to feel mildly disturbed by the newfound realization.

Then I studied his expression, his visible affection, and the way he looked at me like my opinion mattered. He made it so I didn't mind that I cared about him this fast. He also made it easy to support him, to release this man, confident he'll be back.

"Yes, I do." I leaned forward on my tiptoes, still naked, kissing his stubbled chin.

Something else was on the tip of his tongue, something more personal he itched to tell me. I waited, drowning in his clever eyes for seconds, minutes, hours.

In the end, he kept it to himself.

Before I pulled up my big girl pants, masked the frustration I had no intention of letting him observe, Emmanuel grasped my jaw in his palms.

Hands that invent. Hands that cure, I reminded myself. *Let him do his thing.*

"I'll be back late the next few days." He dragged me into a mind-numbing kiss. His teeth nibbled on my bottom lip, followed by his tongue drowning past my teeth, tangling in mine.

Emmanuel's half-moan, half-groan rattled my bones. His promise crowded over every negative feeling that had crept into my heart.

"You're mine." He pressed his forehead to mine. "I'll be back late every night. I won't fuck with your sleep, but I will come back for our cookie date once we're done. Hopefully by the weekend. Almost absolutely."

"Will you call?" I hated that my voice had this desperate, weak ring to it, regardless of how hard I tried to rein it in.

I'll Be Watching You

My Seraphine's voice had been a result of years of practice, second nature, really. I'd always been in control of my vocal cords. I wasn't used to hearing it uncontrollably feeble outside my non-consent-themed podcasts.

Then again, nothing about Emmanuel and the lightning-fast, nose-dive falling for him had been.

"Three days without your voice?" He pulled back, cocking an eyebrow. "Talking to me? Never."

That's all it took to sedate my limbs and calm my racing heart.

Except—as I ended up finding out the hard way—it hasn't been enough.

Not by a mile. Not by a thousand of them.

I step out of my bedroom, strolling over to where I spent the majority of the last Emmanuel-lacking days. My living room.

"Hmm." My sigh pours from my lips as I play with the three yellow daffodils he'd gotten me.

They were gifts he left by my door each night, my stalking lover. On the second day, I told him fuck my sleep and he, in return, surprised me by laughing. He obviously still said no.

Remembering his laughter brings joy to my heart, only to be overrun quickly by self-doubt. It's the sliver of insecurities that travels up my spine, curling its sly claws around my nape.

Maybe the flowers and the distance are Emmanuel's way of telling me he isn't ready for this yet. Maybe the voyeur in him trumps over the side that wants a relationship that said such sweet words I've been eager to believe.

Because while work isn't fake, the letting me rest part might have been.

No.

Yes.

Maybe?

My brows knead together in concentration, forcing the voices to shut the hell up. I'm a grown woman. If this dating-relationship thing is going to last, I'll have to ask Emmanuel what is what, instead of jumping to conclusions.

I've experienced rejection one too many times, that it's highly possible I'm projecting on Emmanuel.

Which he doesn't deserve. Nope. I'll talk to him about it today.

It's still pretty early on this Saturday morning, around nine a.m. give or take, for him to be up after the week he had. When I spare a glance in the direction of the apartment in front of me, I see it's empty.

As much as I miss him, I'm aware of how cruel it'd be to wake Emmanuel up now. Sure, I could go about it in the subtle, happy-ending kind of way. I could do the whole trench-coat-and-nothing-underneath surprise.

At the images my brain conjures, my breasts grow heavy picturing his drowsy, sleepy eyes. How

I'll Be Watching You

they'd widen when I'd drop down to my knees the second he opened the door.

The scene kicks off in my head, the salty taste of his precum coating my tongue as though I'm there on his floor, taking him in my mouth, deep throating him to make up for the lost time.

It's an option.

But he needs his sleep.

Without him here and the frustration rearing its ugly head to ruin the love I have for him, I'm left returning to my daffodils for comfort. They're smooth, and I hate that they're like this.

I wish the flower would come to life and somehow sink its nonexistent teeth in me. Just to feel something, any sort of pain to remind me of Emmanuel's harsh touch.

Anything.

I'm going nuts.

I need to get out of here.

I've hibernated for three whole days. The cookies I baked are chilling for Emmanuel. I've been attempting and failing to record something, anything, that I even refused Liberty's offer for lunch.

It's time to do something else since this clearly isn't working.

Before heading out, I check the weather. I'm sure the temperature dropped during the days I haven't bothered to air the apartment—gross and very unlike me, but I just wasn't in the mood.

Now that I open the window, I feel the gust of wind whipping at my hair, freezing me in a matter of seconds. Quickly, I pull the window shut, wrapping my hands on the opposite arms, and scurry to my bedroom.

I won't survive a trip around the neighborhood without proper clothes, so I go for what I consider my fall fashion. I throw on a pair of light jeans, a crimson long-sleeve T-shirt, same color sweater and sneakers, and a white wool hat, leaving my hair down.

"Ready to brace the day," I say to my reflection, smiling a genuine smile. I should've done it yesterday, before that even, I'm aware. I've been stupid to be holed up here.

"No more negative talk, missy. Better late than never." My smile broadens. Talking to oneself can be so uplifting sometimes that I don't understand why people don't do it more often.

The joy of the concept of a day outside followed by meeting Emmanuel paints my world in every color, that nothing can ruin it. I hum KALEO's, "Way Down We Go," the song Emmanuel chose for us the first night we had our neighbor-sex, I like to call it, uplifting my mood up another two or ten notches.

I'll Be Watching You

Manhattan is epically gorgeous this morning, I notice as I step outside to the pavement. Orange hues rule the shop decorations, the leaf colors, and the clothes and accessories of nearly everyone around me.

Early risers in windbreakers jog past our neighborhood, people sipping on their drinks in the small cafés—mostly pumpkin spice, I can tell if I look closely. The rest stroll peacefully, as if they appreciate these precious, quiet moments in our city.

Sweet scents of flowers from the florist to my right waft in my direction. I turn toward the shop, about to walk inside to revel in another dose of colors and inhale the smells before I grab my own latte bagel and start strolling around SoHo.

I take one step, just one.

An arm around my belly fastens my back to a man's thin, flat chest, his hand clasping around my mouth to keep my scream bottled inside and not rip out into the street.

My heart lurches against my chest; my eyes widen in terror.

I'm about to signal for someone to help me. I mean, even in New York a flailing woman being mouth gagged by a stranger wouldn't be ignored, would she?

Or kick. I could kick him.

Except… I don't want to.

I don't *have* to.

Eva Marks

With his rough, familiar voice in my ear, pressing to the small of my back his cock that I dreamt about for three days, my whole body relaxes on command.

Whatever's good in this world becomes fantastically great in an instant when Emmanuel's rough voice whispers in my ear, "Going somewhere without me, songbird?"

CHAPTER FOURTEEN
Emmanuel

Not an ounce of shame clings to me for stalking Sloane. Not a hint of remorse. Nothing.

I'm too turned on and missed her way too much to give a shit.

After the week I had, who could blame me?

There isn't a breathing soul who would for acting like this.

Judging by the hushed moan Sloane lets out on my palm restricting her lips and how her muscles lose the tension in them, she won't either.

"You thought I wasn't coming for you?" I slide my hand to the side of her neck as an elderly lady slows her walk to eye me as though she's about to beat me with her umbrella.

"I-I—" The sentence is stuck in Sloane's throat, but it isn't distress tugging on her vocal cords. It's arousal.

Eva Marks

The moan gave her away, and so did her ruddy cheeks. Her back arching an inch to pin her ass tighter to my steel-hard cock is a massive clue too.

Surreptitiously—as much as a man can whilst leading a woman in broad daylight in a possessive grip—I drag her back into my building, punching in the code to get us inside.

My intention for the day was to catch her out on the street, then join her on this trip she intended to take by herself. Which we will after I taste her in ways that will, with absolute certainty, have someone call the police on us.

"Thought I haven't missed you?" Next to the flight of stairs, where no curious passerby will be able to see us, I pin her to the renovated tile wall.

Her back slams into it; her arms go limp at her sides. Her complacent behavior is there for me. These gestures are meant to encourage me to continue this game we're playing, to grab ahold of the situation, do with her as I will.

"That I wasn't losing my mind every second of every day that I haven't sunk my cock into one of your holes and made you scream my name?" I bracket her face, a palm on each side of it, while my nose dips to the slope of her neck, skating my lips on it, inhaling her.

"Emmanuel." She tilts her head to the side, allowing me easier access. "I know you have."

I'll Be Watching You

"Then?" With a tilt of my head, I examine her like she's more prey than the woman I spent days yearning for.

Suddenly, I'm aware that, despite being away from the street, one of my neighbors could walk in on us at any given moment. Being the subject of observation usually wouldn't lead to my dick straining in my pants and my breaths coming out shallow. I'm the man on the other side of the looking glass.

But not today. Sloane's warm body trembles beneath me, her eyes—now dark and wanting—stare at me helplessly. This sight, this feeling of her, it's home.

Fuck anyone who walks in on us. Let them watch.

I grind my erection to her soft belly, lower my lips to hers, and suck on the seductive, pink flesh.

"Talk to me." I pin her harder to the wall one last time, smirking as I pull back to gauge her expression.

"I didn't want to wake you." Sloane's sweater stretches across her full breasts on an inhale, her soft breath caressing my face when the air travels out. "You were up this whole time?"

The quiver in her voice, the crinkling around her eyes and mouth are telltales of unwarranted insecurities.

"I was." Acting fast, I grip her chin before her head bows. "I didn't lie to you when I said I'd come for you today. But I've…"

It's too much; her scent, clean and fresh, and her lips so close to mine. I can't keep talking, I want to kiss her so bad. Then again, I do owe her explanations and honesty. Mostly, since I don't want to witness this look of doubt ever again.

"I'll explain everything." Our lips brush as I speak. "First, though, I have to love you."

Sloane whimpers something, the equivalent of an agreement. It's all the *yes* I need for me to descend upon her, demanding her lips for another kiss, more intense, more bestial. My songbird melts where I possess her, giving away the parts of her I'm all too keen to claim.

My hand slips up the curve of her waist to cup her breast, molding it, feeling how fucking real it is. It's only when she slips hers between us to undo my jeans that I halfway wake up.

Connecting us by pressing my mouth to her forehead, I whisper, "So, where did you really want to go today, my love?"

A low tremor causes her body to shiver softly, tenderly. Much like everything about her. "On a walk."

"Mind if I join you?" I draw back, running my thumb on her bottom lip that's swollen from kissing.

I'll Be Watching You

Her mouth curves into a smile and she inhales, almost in relief. "Please."

It's a strange feeling, to be needed the way she needs me.

I've been needed at work—my expertise, my opinions, my signature—and at home helping my mother around the house or giving my father a hand when the car won't start. Even on one of my occasional fucks, they called me to help them reach their climax.

But it's never been like this. Never with such affection, never asking me to be there simply because of…me.

Strange feeling, though not at all unwelcome.

Mainly, since I really need her like this too.

"After you, then." Putting more distance between us, I adjust my jeans. "Wherever you go, I'll follow."

Her eyes glimmer, a hint of mischief flaring behind them. I don't have to suspect what she's thinking; we're no longer engulfed by a haze of lust, and her mind has cleared at this point. She doesn't guess—she *knows* it's no accident that I'm here.

For once in my life, I'm not embarrassed or apprehensive about it. Moreover, I have every intention of telling her the truth.

Our fingers interlace on their own accord, my thumb stroking the inside of her wrist as if I've done it forever.

"Let's go." Sloane tugs on my hand, pulling me away from the smells of dust and out into the street.

The gray fall skies greet us when we walk out alongside a new wave of people who weren't here ten minutes ago. We navigate between them while they walk past us or into corner shops, organic breakfast restaurants, or the buildings, carrying grocery bags.

Sloane doesn't stop for any of those.

I watch her watch everyone around us, smiling at children or eyeing that flower shop she was about to visit, but she doesn't stop.

Asking her why or where she's guiding us will break the charm surrounding the mystery destination. Besides, studying her in silence does it for me, so this situation suits me perfectly.

When the street parts into a fork, Sloane heads straight up and into the triangular park in the center of it. Though it's nowhere near the greenery of Central Park—especially since we're still standing on pavement instead of grass—the trees planted around the park and their orange leaves are a nice separation from the outside world.

"This is it." She pauses next to a stone bench in the center of everything. Hesitation and excitement mingle on her face in the form of a shy smile, her body swaying side to side. "Is that okay?"

"I wouldn't want to sit anywhere else." I nod, and we occupy one of the benches.

I'll Be Watching You

I'm not being gallant. Not doing anything against my will by being a yes man just to appease her. If this is where she wants to be, no one could convince me there's a better spot in the entire world.

A kid sprints from one side of the park to the other. Both his dads hold hands, smile at each other in that knowing parent-smile, then stand up from the adjacent bench and stroll over to him where he waits near the humming street.

I study the picture of the happy family.

Will I ever have mine?

Since when did I want one?

"You spied on me." Her voice and her foot that's playing with mine lure me out of my thoughts.

Straight to the point. As am I. "Yes."

"You didn't come for me, though." Another accurate observation, except this one has sadness laced into it.

Despite my need to be honest with her, I'm stuck. The sudden fear of rejection sinks into me, so I settle for a short sentence and a show of affection. Whatever I can do to keep her here.

"I did, eventually." I tilt my head, lifting her knuckles to my lips.

"Yes." She casts her bronze eyes to the floor. In the simple gesture, she tells me she has more to say. More like I hurt her.

Seeing my current approach fail, I change my approach. Her pain makes me stronger in my need to protect her, even if she ends up walking away while thinking I'm a depraved fuck.

I grip her chin, forcing her eyes to mine. "I'm going to be honest, Sloane."

Hope simmers into her gaze. "Okay."

"You know who I am, right? *How* I am." To be perfectly clear, I level my eyes with hers, lowering my voice a notch. "I like watching. I like doing it from the shadows."

"Yes, I know."

"I've been this person for nearly twenty years." I inhale through my nose, the scents of Sloane, smoke, and something sweet from around us carrying to me with it. "There's no big trauma or secret involved. My mom didn't threaten me that masturbating will guarantee my ticket to hell, and I wasn't molested or have a warped perception of the idea of a healthy sex life. I am this way just because. And I won't change."

"I don't want to change you." She wraps her palm around mine, sliding my hand to her cheek. "I love you. For the man that you are. Exactly who and how you are."

Her words are a stab landing right at my heart. Not because the feeling isn't mutual, or because they sound ingenuine. It's the sincerity pouring from them that scares me. She's so sure, and yet has no idea who this man she claims to love is.

"But?" I ask when her eyes talk to me instead of her pouty, beautiful mouth.

I'll Be Watching You

Her heavy sigh pains me. Her next question hits me right in the gut.

"You said you missed me. Did you really, though? I… I'm not passing judgment or anything. I love to think how your eyes are on me even when you're away. It's just, after three days,"—her whole face scrunches, beautiful eyes glistening—"I wouldn't have been able to wait for a second if I were in your shoes. Would've run to you so fast if I would've seen you in your apartment."

"Songbird…"

"Don't." She turns to the other side, escaping my lips when I lean in to kiss her. "You don't have to comfort me. I'm a big girl. And…it was a dumb question to begin with. I'm sorry for asking. You did come for me. I have no idea why I'm being this clingy."

"You're not clingy. Nothing like that." That statement is stupid. I need to do better. "You're special."

The pulsing, constant self-doubt at the back of my mind doesn't deter me from pulling her to me. I lean into her, claiming that kiss I was after. A brief, soft press of my lips to convey how much I care about her.

"I'm not." The signs of concern slowly disappear off her face, but not as fast as I'd like.

"Yeah, you are." I smile to reassure her. "I can't let you go. I don't know that I will even if you tell me to."

My eyes drift to a point behind her, aware of how fucked up my next sentence will be. "I'll do everything for you, Sloane. This other side of me, though? The watching, the stalking…it's a part of who I am. It's not good nor bad, but it's there, just like the color of my eyes and the shape of my nose. That's simply how it is."

The silence between us coaxes me to look at her again. Her lips are twisted, and I notice her palm doesn't grip mine as tightly. I keep to myself while she sorts out what's bothering her.

I was aware that bringing it up will lead to a loaded conversation. My past, my tendencies, the secrets I've told no one but her, they're a lot to hear in one sitting.

Seconds pass, and for some inexplicable reason, regardless of the trepidation that returns to her face for the second time, she's still here.

She's still considering *us*.

I wish I could be as patient as she is. Wish I could wait for all the pieces to be put together for her. Except I can't.

"Talk to me, Sloane." I squeeze her relaxed hand. "You can tell me anything."

"I really prefer not to." She shies away from me a second time.

I'll Be Watching You

I cover her jaw with my palm, pulling her right back. "Talk. To. Me."

"I'm not the jealous type."

The screaming, happy kid storms back in our direction, getting picked up by the raven-haired father at the last minute. It's at that moment that I decide I *will* have that, that I'll do anything in my power to build this life with her.

"I don't care if you are. I would, however, be happy to demolish those insecurities by telling you the truth." Releasing her chin, I cup both her cheeks, holding her possessively. "I can't do that when you don't tell me what's wrong."

She tips her chin up, gazing at me behind thick eyelashes. "I'm not judging you, either."

"We've already established that."

"Other women," she whispers, then blurts out, "does voyeurism mean there'll be other women after we get serious too? When you see me day in, day out and I'm not exciting anymore?"

It takes biting the inside of my cheek to restrain my shocked expression. She's not being ridiculous, nor is the question unreasonable. Nothing like that.

It's her insinuation that makes my eyes widen in surprise. She's perfect in every sense of the word. I can't even begin to fathom how she'd think there's anyone better than her.

Eva Marks

"You will *never* bore me." I rip her hat off and thread my fingers through her hair, massaging her scalp and slowly bringing her to my lips.

"You can't say that."

"I can and I will." Talking with my mouth a hairsbreadth from hers, with our breaths mingled and her short rasps making my dick hard, I whisper, "I've watched you for two years. Two years of you scratching your belly, of you doing house chores, of your sweet voice talking about changing sheets or moaning in pleasure. Only. You. I've never been, nor will I ever be, bored of you."

She leans in to kiss me, and I allow it for a brief second.

"I could not believe my fucking luck, having found you in real life." A tear escapes her, catching at my palm. "No one comes close to you. Never have, never will."

Her insecurities still hover in her expression.

I'll be damned if anything will stop me before I squash the doubts from her mind.

"You're the songbird I came home to for many, many nights, Sloane." I lower my voice further since there are children everywhere. "The woman I beat off to, the woman I envisioned saving, as having as *mine*. That's why I didn't run to you this morning like any other man would. I took joy in stalking you just as much as I'd take in fucking you. Soon."

I'll Be Watching You

Realization and lust change intermittently behind her eyes.

"Soon?"

"Unless you'd like to stay here."

"No." Sloane stands up, clutching her hat in one hand, reaching for mine with the other. "I want to go."

I don't waste time, don't bother to breathe before I join her.

And give her the full extent of my somber expression.

"My good girl knows better than to make demands." My jaw tics, my body emanating authority. "You want something? You beg for it."

"Daddy." She doesn't hesitate, not for a second. "Please."

CHAPTER FIFTEEN
Sloane

"We're not going home?" I ask Emmanuel when he starts leading us in the opposite direction after the brisk approving nod he spared my way.

He glances at me without breaking his stride, his blue eyes holding a million dirty secrets. "No."

Without another piece of information, not a single hint, I'm curious. I'm also hot and aching for him, so the truth is it doesn't really matter where he's taking me, as long as we're together.

My desperation runs so deep that if Emmanuel shoved me this minute into a dark alley or abandoned building to fuck on the stairwell, I wouldn't have hesitated to do just that.

"Okay." Unable to restrain myself, I press myself closer to his side, rising on my tiptoes to whisper, "Daddy."

I'll Be Watching You

Dried leaves crunch under our feet, people chat to our left and right, but somehow, Emmanuel's growl trumps them all in its volume and frequency.

How could I think for a second this man hasn't missed me?

I knew he stalked me, walked to the front of my apartment long after I fell asleep for three nights in a row. He put flowers there not to remind me of his existence—to make a point that he'd been watching me.

Everything has been laid out for me to see all along. I just have to trust him.

While I'm daydreaming about him, Emmanuel veers us into the subway on Canal Street, his descent cool and calculated despite the heat that pours out of every cell in his body.

"I don't have my MetroCard on me," I say at the turnstiles.

"No need." He swipes his, signaling for me to pass.

I turn midway to ask how he's going to get in when I see him plucking another card from his jeans pocket.

"It's extremely sexy that you're this prepared for everything." My Seraphine's voice slithers into my words.

Emmanuel doesn't correct me this time. In fact, he says nothing at all. Remaining silent, he claims my hand again to guide us down another flight of stairs, then pulls us to the stop on the left.

Since I've gotten acquainted with another side of him today, I know he's not mad at my slip-up. I notice it in the way his thumb strokes my wrist, how his intense gaze slides over my body while we wait for the engine to pull the brakes in our stop.

So, between the throngs of people and the whooshes of hot air, as other lines fly by us, I tease my broody lover a little more.

"Truth is, there isn't a single thing about you that doesn't turn me on." I spin to press my chest to his, locking my hands behind his neck.

"Sloane…"

His warning has the opposite effect of what I'm sure he intended. It's true I want to be his good girl and do whatever he asks. I also have a tingling eagerness to find out how he'll punish me for being bad.

"Your kneaded eyebrows and creased forehead, too." I lean on my tiptoes, talking against the curve of his neck and nuzzling my nose to it. "All they do is ruin my panties with how wet and desperate I am for you. My bra feels so tight on my breasts, my nipples are painfully hard that I think they're two seconds from poking a hole in my pads—"

The screeching behind me announces a train stopping. Emmanuel untangles himself from my

I'll Be Watching You

hands deftly, then moves one of his to curl around my nape in a possessive gesture.

He barely waits for the passengers inside the cart to get out before giving me the tiniest push to enter first.

My blood swarms inside my veins and reaches everywhere. It's in my beating heart, pouring over to fuel the excitement in my belly, rushing to my clit, making it thrum.

I wasn't lying when I teased him. I really do love any and every aspect of Emmanuel. Every last bit of him.

Then again, if it awakens the feral side in him, I start planning another taunting session on our ride to wherever it is he's taking me. I start, and I fail.

"You want me to fuck you right here in the subway?" Emmanuel's thin yet powerful frame crowds my vision as he shoves me against the back of the cart.

"I-I—"

Imitating what he did in his building, Emmanuel's hands cage me on both sides of my head. His palm presses firmly on the rattling glass. His breath is hot, scorching my skin, his teeth grazing the place where my shoulder meets my neck.

"I've never been on the exhibitionist side until I met you." The hoarseness in his voice steals my breath away. "But trust me, little songbird, I'm a real fast learner."

"Miss, are you all right?" A tall woman walks up to us, standing behind Emmanuel.

My humor and arousal drain from me in a heartbeat.

And I hate it. Because my heart and soul need Emmanuel. I'm seconds from melting into Emmanuel's domineering, all-consuming presence and I hate having anyone in the way.

But submitting to him completely isn't an option right now.

The woman has her hand in her bag, probably searching for either a pepper spray or cell phone. Neither of the options bodes well for Emmanuel.

My eyes dance between him and her at rapid speed, while his ravenous ones are fixed on me and nothing else.

I slide beneath him, my movements swift before he'll grab my wrist, and then everything will go to shit. Raising my arms and pulling my teeth into the widest smile I can manage, I say, "I'm fine, that's my boyfriend. We were…excited."

Emmanuel has turned around amid my *Nothing to see here* speech. He's staring at me as well. Yes, he's behind me, and yes, I sense both things. It's our connection combined with Emmanuel's intensity, gaping a hole through my back, they're so fierce.

It's his hand around my waist that tips me off too.

I'll Be Watching You

An insane blush creeps up my cheeks at his attention, at him hearing me say first the word *boyfriend*.

We haven't put a title on what we have together. *I love you* doesn't have to mean anything. It doesn't put me on edge, the commitment, but who knows whether we're in the same headspace or not?

Maybe his *I love you* is more of a *you're a great fuck, a nice person, and great to look at, so let's test the waters for now*?

It could be. Then again, when I gauge the woman's reaction, how while the train stops, she drops whatever she was holding and her hand returns threat-free, I relax.

I did what was right. If Emmanuel has issues with my wording, coaxing the woman to go away will be how I'll backtrack from the boyfriend title.

"Phew." The kind stranger's mouth curls up, a contrast to her tight-lipped expression a second ago. "Good. Every assault on a woman is worse than a shotgun to my heart."

She has to be around sixty years old, slender, and somewhat fragile, and still, she came for me. It was brave of her to approach someone in such a menacing stance such as Emmanuel's, such a selfless act I have to show her my appreciation even though I wasn't in any danger.

"You're absolutely right." I sneak back toward Emmanuel—who on cue hugs me tighter and plants a tender kiss on my cheek. "Thank you."

"Anytime." With an elegant spin, she heads toward one of the available seats to read something on her phone.

"Where were we?" Emmanuel growls in my ear, his erection pushing against my back. "Scratch that. I don't care."

"W-what do you care about?" Dread coats my voice, aware he'll demand an explanation. Or worse, confirm my worries that he never meant *I love you* like I did.

"Look at me."

My head swivels slowly to face him, the day-old scruff grazing my cheek.

"Boyfriend?" he prods.

I'm absolutely freaking positive my cheeks run crimson red at this point. Somehow, I manage to utter my prepared speech in a whisper, "It was the best wording I had to calm her down, that's it."

"Is that so?" He pulls me infinitely harder to his chest, his steel-blue eyes eating up my profile.

"Yes, of course," I blurt out. "I didn't assume we were or anything."

"Hmm," is all he gives me at the exact moment the train stops at 59 & Lex.

He laces our fingers together, pulling me after him out of the train and up the stairs into the street.

I'll Be Watching You

Once we're out, he moves us to the side, standing inches from me as he silently takes my hat and fixes it on my hair.

The mixture of curiosity and doubt form a dangerous concoction that threatens to explode in my stomach. I have to ask, "What does hmm mean?"

"You didn't assume anything." His penetrative glare challenges the cold wind, melting me to the concrete as though it were lava. "You called it exactly like it is. You are my girlfriend, Sloane. More than that—and those are words I'll repeat over and over—you. Are. Mine."

I whimper. I fucking whimper, my knees wobbling in the middle of Manhattan. My strong *boyfriend* catches on to it, cupping my cheeks while dragging me to his firm body for a kiss.

"Mine," he whispers. "Say it."

"Yours," I tell him, but when it comes out too weak, I draw strength from the man who's becoming my everything and repeat with vehemence, "*Yours.*"

CHAPTER SIXTEEN
Emmanuel

My office and the labs I manage at GeneOrg are my own private kingdom.

They belong to me not for bland reasons, like being Jalen Arsenault, the genius scientist and businessman who built the company, or for the shares I own.

The high-end facilities, the people in them, and the work we do are mine because they're sacred to me. Since Jalen approached me all those years ago, his mission became my mission.

No outsider, journalist, or even spouses have been allowed in the corridors I walk through on this peaceful Saturday morning with Sloane. No one but her.

I trust her. It's too soon. This complete and utter confidence in her is neither substantiated nor warranted. She's done nothing to gain my trust that

I'll Be Watching You

she won't touch anything, secretly photograph our secrets, and distribute or tell anyone about our life's work.

And yet it doesn't fucking matter.

When I catch her curious eyes and excited smile from the corner of my eye, I don't need her to have earned anything. I'm sure as the morning's sky is blue that this woman wouldn't do a single thing to betray me.

"Em." Her voice severs me from my thoughts, seducing me back to reality.

"Yes, songbird?" I slow us on our way to my office, checking the labs' conditions out of habit.

"Umm, not that I'm not appreciative of you bringing me here."

She stops when I stop at the doorway to my office. I don't punch in the code, the first step before swiping the employee card I carry in my wallet at all times.

"Please, continue." I stand there, expecting her to finish the sentence she started.

Inside the room where I'm authorized to manually turn off the CCTV cameras—which I did during our ride up in the elevators—her talking will no longer be a viable option. I have plans for her, and each one includes her speaking only when I say so.

Her lips scrunch, her feet shifting left, then right. "I thought," she says in a hushed tone, "you wanted to have sex?"

Eva Marks

Lifting her chin with a firm grip, I bend my head to hers, my lips coasting on her cheek. "Oh, we're definitely fucking, little Sloane. This lab nerd is gonna fuck you in his office long and hard. I'll break your sweet pussy in two, ruin it for any other man."

The skin on my cheek lights on fire from her gasp, my cock jerking with how turned on I am by her.

"By the time I'm done with you, my love,"—my teeth scrape her earlobe, one hand clutching around her waist when she squirms beneath me—"you'll no longer doubt how badly I want you, how *mine* you are."

I still loom over her, nipping the sensitive skin as I reach out to blindly press three-five-six-two-one-asterisk, sliding my card next. The door beeps, cracking open, and I pull Sloane to my chest, then move us both inside the room.

"You're not a nerd," she peeps while I unbutton and unzip her once we're in the office.

"But I very much am." I'm not ashamed of it, even less now that I'm cognizant of how much she likes the man that I am.

"Facts don't offend me." I shove the automated door closed, grateful for the walls I left frosted on Friday night.

My free hand roams down Sloane's belly, unbuttoning and unzipping her jeans, then toying on the edge of her waistband, eliciting desperate

I'll Be Watching You

moans from her pouty lips. "*Nothing* offends me when I'm about to have my fingers up to the knuckles in your dripping wet cunt."

Her cry echoes through the walls as I penetrate her slick opening. Besides being closed off to the world, my office is also soundproof so no one will eavesdrop on information not intended for them to hear.

It's hard to believe Sloane would mind Henry the security guard listening in on us, but I do. It's one thing when it's her work, at her studio, while she's fulfilling her dreams and making a living at the same time. I'm proud of her for the woman she is.

When it's us, though, Sloane's moans, cries, and everything in between belongs to me, nobody else.

"You like my fingers inside you, baby?" I push her jeans lower with the hand that's not busy pleasuring my woman. With the constraints of her jeans gone, I have more room to pinch and flick her slick clit, to make her beg louder for me. "Like how I rub those tight walls, stroking that hard little bundle of nerves?"

"God, yes." Her head tilts up, her hat scrunching on her head. She doesn't gaze in that direction, however. She's looking at me hungrily through lust-filled, hooded eyes. "Please don't stop."

"I won't, not until you come. But you should know something." I keep pumping her with my hand as I bend to my knees. "My body won't be the only thing you'll come to today."

"Wha—" Sloane's question gets swallowed back in her throat the second I part her folds and my lips lock in on her pink mound, sucking on it hard. "Oh. Oh!"

Adding a fourth finger, I stretch her out while licking, nipping, and kissing her sensitive spot. She grinds her hips on my face, one of her hands sneaking to my hair, drawing my face to her.

I separate myself from her, glowering at my songbird's parted lips and wanting expression. "Who's in charge here, Sloane?"

She gulps in what might appear like fear, but it really isn't. Her arousal is evident, her thighs clenching on my fingers.

"Who?" I growl.

"You, Daddy," she whispers, taking her head back.

"Very good." Backing away, I keep thrusting into her. "But you've still been bad, little songbird, and for that, I'm gonna hold on to your orgasm until you strip for me."

It's a hardship for her, pushing from the wall that supports her while her knees are wobbly from my fingers fucking her. My brave girl does it regardless.

Pulling out one hand at a time, she relieves herself of her bulky sweater. Her tight top clings to her body, giving me the view of her round breasts

I'll Be Watching You

rising and falling with the effort to hold herself upright.

She does it for me. The realization swells my heart. My dick too.

"You're doing so well," I praise her, grasping one thigh to encourage her by helping her balance. "So fucking well, my beautiful songbird."

A hint of a smile curls up her lips.

"Are you done, though?" The warmth I had for her obliterates in a snap, the spring in me turning into a harsh winter.

"No, Daddy." Sloane reaches for the hem of her shirt.

"Good girl." I watch her move, my fingers digging deeper into her flesh as my hunger rises. "Don't stop there."

On the shirt's descent to the floor, I catch a whiff of her perfume on her shirt. I don't linger on it, though, my eyes captivated by something far more interesting once Sloane's bra is peeled off her.

She's beautiful. Clothed, and even more so naked. I'll never get my fill of her. Her luscious, seductive curves on the background of my cold office clash like two polar opposites that form a complete picture.

And it belongs to me.

"That's it." Placing a firm hand on her belly, I pin her back to the wall. My tongue swirls around her swollen clit in teasing ministrations, my lips taking a break to say, "I want you to do one last thing for me."

"Anything." She squirms in place, each syllable out of her mouth jagged in her effort. "Anything, I'll do anything you ask me to."

"When you orgasm all over my tongue, songbird,"—I draw my thumb over her lips. looking at every inch of her pussy—"when you come, you sing for me at the top of your fucking lungs."

"Yes, oh, God, anyth—"

The rest of whatever Sloane started to say transforms into a song rather than coherent speech. She might not be a singer, not formally, but the sounds her lungs produce are purely melodic.

While I lick and suck, finger fuck her and stretch her open for what's coming next, I gaze up at her. I take in the change in her expression, from heated to desperate to fighting against rolling her eyes when her climax is too much to contain.

"Come," I say, pumping her deeper, stroking her G-spot. "Now."

A flick of my tongue is the only push she needs. The guttural voice reverberating through the room isn't that of a symphony anymore. She screams my name like it's beaten out of her, and with my fingers fucking her hard to squeeze out the last of her orgasm, it's as close to the truth as it gets.

"I'm so turned on from eating your pussy, baby." Not giving her a chance to recuperate, I throw her

I'll Be Watching You

shoes to the side, rid her of the jeans and toss my jacket somewhere behind me. "Just as much as I love fucking you."

I stand up to grab under her thighs. Her legs and hands curl around me, her breasts grazing the thin fabric of my T-shirt.

"Are you going to fuck me in one of your labs?" Her eyes twinkle, gold specks of mischief sparkling behind them like crackling flames.

"You'd want that, wouldn't you?"

She lets me manhandle her however I like it when I lead us to the back of my office.

"Yes." Her voice is breathy and excited in tandem.

"Greedy little slut." We make it to my desk. I round it to where my chair and lab coat are, dropping Sloane on the wooden surface.

I wipe the contents of the desk off its wooden surface; pens, pencils, a cup I left over the weekend, and papers for me to sign. They crash on the ceramic tiles on the floor in a series of loud bangs. A total wonderful, perfect calamity.

While this mess goes on around her, Sloane sits there in silence, her legs spread around me, her pussy slick and dripping on my sacred workspace.

"Take my cock out, little Sloane."

She does it immediately. Her hands slip the button out, unzipping me, drawing my boxers down. She moans when she wraps her fingers around my girth, legs parting wider, her ass moving to the edge of the desk.

"That's it." Her hair is softer than silk as I coil it in a punishing grip, and I mark her neck with an equally unforgiving bite. "The labs, though, are the one thing I can't give you. Do you understand?"

"Okay." She doesn't sound disappointed, just fists my dick harder, squeezing a bead of precum from the throbbing head.

"You'd take whatever I throw your way, wouldn't you?" I bruise her shoulder by sucking harder on it. "As long as I fuck you."

"As long,"—she pants, breathless—"as long as you'll love me."

I had no idea this was the answer I wanted—no, *needed* to hear. But it is. Fuck, how it's exactly the words I burned for.

And I'll tell her that. After I pleasure the living fuck out of her.

I shove her back to the emptied desk and turn for a second to retrieve the item I'm about to use on her.

"Emmanuel?"

"Yes?" I ask, looking back at her.

"I know I'm not supposed to make requests while we…"

"You aren't." Spinning back, I lift one of her legs, spanking her ass once, then her pussy. A profound, depraved satisfaction consumes me from

I'll Be Watching You

hearing the sound of her screams. "However, now that you've been punished for it, little songbird, tell me."

"The lab coat." She bites her bottom lip, one breath heaving after the other. "Please, Daddy, please wear it while you're fucking me."

"So filthy." I slap her pussy again as I stroke the length of my cock, coaxing a tortured moan to burst from her lips. "I will. Put your feet on the desk, open wider, and lie still like the good girl you are."

"Yes, Daddy," she says.

I cast my eyes on the view of her shifting, spreading herself for me.

And then I start.

CHAPTER SEVENTEEN
Sloane

A low humming makes my clit flutter. Sweet with anticipation to have him take me wearing his lab coat while still a bit sore, the touch of pain from Emmanuel's slap a reminder of whom I belong to.

Daddy.

"Remember I said you won't just be fucked by me today?"

He has his back to me, blocking the sight of what he's doing. But I don't have to see it; in the silence of the office, I hear it. The *whoosh* of a spray is a whisper slashing through the air, the scent of a disinfectant wafting to my nose.

"Y-yes." I'm experiencing a mixture of excitement and hesitancy, not the least bit scared.

Then he turns to face me. In his right hand, there's a small oval object, and on his handsome broody face a sinister smirk slowly emerges. He

I'll Be Watching You

presses a button, and the numbers on the screen begin to run down. Ten seconds, nine, eight… All the way down to zero.

The device vibrates, causing even Emmanuel's strong grip to quiver.

He can't possibly mean…

Oh, yes. The glint in his eyes tells me that he absolutely does.

"Gonna slip this into this pretty, sopping hole of yours."

When the vibrations stop, Emmanuel blindly presses two buttons, and the clock starts counting down from thirty. He strokes his cock in measured movements, his eyes roaming my naked body, my spread legs, how I'm wet, swollen, and greedy for his attention.

It's in these moments that his smirk drowns out, the darkness rising.

It would've intimidated anyone else. Me, I'm falling deeper and harder.

"I'll be holding onto this, choosing when to set it off, how long you'll have to wait." Another step closer. He's looming over me, the number zero closing in fast. "It all depends on whether you're a good girl or not. So, do. Not. Move."

Emmanuel places the buzzing timer on my clit before returning to his chair, leaving me to face this wonderfully cruel device by myself. My teeth sink into the inside of my cheek with the ferocity it takes to stay still, to be worthy of Emmanuel's praise.

From my lying down position, I lower my gaze to see that he hasn't gone out of the room to test me. It's too arousing, too challenging, and scary to do it all by myself.

To my absolute fucking delight, I see that not only he hasn't, but he's sliding into his lab coat like I asked.

The urge to satisfy him intensifies tenfold at the sight. It also makes it a million times more difficult to hold on to the orgasm which is completely and entirely his.

Finally, the timer ceases its beeping and reverberating against my clit. Emmanuel is looking at me again, his coat is open, his slim chest is on display, and his thick dick is hard against his stomach.

"Songbird." He picks up the timer, deftly setting it in his hand without letting his gaze stray from my eyes. "You're being such a well-behaved slut for Daddy."

The concoction of degradation and praise Emmanuel delivers hits all my pleasure points, and his name becomes a shriek and a prayer on my lips.

A strong, fiery buildup stretches and tightens my body. I'm a human bomb, prepped to explode at his words spoken in such a husky, ominous voice.

I'll Be Watching You

"You know you are." Emmanuel's thumb stretches my navel ring, then coasts on the area where the timer sat. My hips buckle in response to the sensitive areas he's toying with. "No, no, no. Good girls don't move, do they?"

"No, Daddy," I choke out.

Unlike before, I can't see the numbers on the screen anymore. I definitely won't be able to gauge them when Emmanuel sinks the device into my slit.

My hands flatten on the wooden table, the invasion almost too much to bear.

"That's it." He shoves it in deeper, pushing it to my upper walls while probing my asshole with the tip of his cock. "Take it, Sloane. Take it with my dick teasing your ass, with my thumb on your clit."

Emmanuel continues to push the timer inside until I groan like a wounded animal when he finds the spot that has me crying for him.

"Look at me." His growl is a command I rush to obey. "I'd say you have three seconds left,"—he rubs my aching mound just as he promised—"get ready."

I want to. I try.

I'm dying to be able to please him, and fuck, I really wish I could.

Then the quivering sensation pummels into me, attacking me from inside, burning the rope I'm barely balancing on as is. My pucker is soaked from my juices, and Emmanuel uses it to enter me slightly, not enough to hurt but more than plenty to elicit an unimaginable flare of desire.

"Em, please," I beg, knowing how close I am to snapping. "Please, I need to, I have to…"

"Hold it." The pressure of his cock is gone. Instead of letting go, he rubs me like he would a real vibrator, spreading the pleasure inside my pussy. "One more second…"

Years of working in a lab have gotten Emmanuel acquainted with the timings of the wonderfully demonic device, the way he plans his tortures. The instant the timer's beeping and thrumming stops, Emmanuel whips it out of me, impaling me with his cock instead.

"Now," he thunders. "Be a good fucking girl,"— he rams into my pussy; his steely blue eyes plow into mine harder than his thrusts—"and come."

The orgasm rips through me, deconstructing me into a million tiny pieces, though not for long. Through the unyielding strength of Emmanuel's grasp on one of my thighs and the lust-filled gaze he pins me down with, I'm being glued back together into one gasping, clawing, better human.

"My beautiful Sloane." He slides his shaft out, pounding back mercilessly. "Looks like my desk is going to be stained with your orgasm."

I'm too dazed, satisfied, and full to care. It doesn't seem like it bothers him, either. Emmanuel continues to rock into me in fierce thrusts, smacking

I'll Be Watching You

my clit in intervals, impaling me to the point I can sense another climax pushing through me.

The tension coils at the pit of my stomach, and I look at the man who owns me so completely for help.

"You're not sorry?"

My back scratches against the desk from the force of his pounding, as Emmanuel's balls slap against my ass. But he's capable of more. More pain, more dominance. It's right there, behind his eyes. And maybe I need to be a brat to coax it from him.

"Only if you want me to be."

"I see we started talking back." His fingers hurt, breaking skin, driving me to scream out in pain and pleasure. In my peripheral vision, I see him playing with the timer again.

"You want to test me, Sloane?"

"No, Daddy."

"Bad girls don't get to have their pussy vibrating."

He glowers down at me, slanting his body on mine, his taut chest grazing my nipples. His lab coat caresses my waist, the added light touch is barely there, agonizing in its tenderness.

His dick slams into me, his body pressing to mine. "They might not even be allowed to come."

"No, please."

The feeble attempt I make to wriggle my hands and grasp him in a plea dies before I manage to move an inch. Emmanuel exerts his dominance on me, pinning them to the desk without ever letting go of his timer.

"Who do you belong to?"

I already know that, already know beyond a shadow of a doubt that he really, truly wants me, exactly as I am and no one else.

I still give him what he asked for. "You."

"Yes, Sloane," he grunts. "Don't you ever forget that you're mine."

"I won't, I promise." The impending orgasm transforms into almost physical pain. "I-I need to come."

"Beg for it." His forehead brushes mine, sweat coating our bodies that slide and glue to one another. "Beg me with your words, tell me how much you want me to pleasure you."

"I'm begging," I gasp, battling to talk despite my tight lungs. "I need you so bad. You're the only one, Emmanuel, the only one who can make me come."

"That's a good girl."

He bites my bottom lip, the hand holding the timer slithering between us. He leaves it on my clit, then overpowers me again, his body weight cramming the device, so it holds still.

"On my count, baby." He grabs one side of my face in his palm, his touch harsh and demanding and oh so perfect.

"Yes, Daddy."

I'll Be Watching You

"Three…" There's no grace in his rhythm anymore, just a pure, animalistic race to claim what's his.

"Two…"

I squeeze my pussy to keep from finding my release before he says *one*.

Emmanuel grunts, fucks me so hard the pain reaches behind my eyes, the unearthly feeling chasing me right behind it.

"One."

As if answering to its master's command, the timer sets off. The quivering sensation carries from my core to the extremities of my body, and I suck in air because the room becomes incredibly closed and tight as Emmanuel's orgasm comes next.

It's him and me here. No floors, no ceiling, no space, no nothing.

Only us.

"My good little songbird." He kisses the tip of my nose, his fingers caressing my cheeks after he tosses the timer aside. "I've never been happier than I am with you."

"Even if I ruined your desk?" I tease.

He answers first by sucking on my lower lip, second by putting a metaphorical lock over my heart so it'll forever be his when he says, "It's not ruined. It's fucking complete now. Just like I am."

CHAPTER EIGHTEEN
Emmanuel

GeneOrg labs and my office—my appreciation for them notwithstanding—are not fit for aftercare, cuddles, or anything warm and fuzzy.

On one hand, it's why I thrive there.

On the other, it means soothing Sloane after being rammed by my lab timer, and by me on the harsh surface of my desk, would be half-assed until we get to her home.

"Coffee, right?" I ask her while loving her through my gaze, still on top of her, still running my finger pads along her cheeks.

Her lips part in confusion, then break into a smile. "Yes, please."

I learned this piece of information much like the rest of what I knew about her. During twenty-four months of listening carefully to her every word, studying her, drinking her in.

I'll Be Watching You

She's been my addiction.

Now, it's much more. Addiction can't even begin to describe what I feel for her these days. Sloane is no longer an outer aspect of my existence; she *is* it, my whole life.

"You'll have anything you want, my little Sloane."

In one swift movement, I shed my lab coat, draping it over her naked body. I scoop her in my arms, and even though her hands are tucked beneath my work attire, she makes an effort to draw me closer to her by pressing her knuckles to my chest.

After placing her gently on the chair, I kiss her messy hair. Our out-of-the-bedroom intimacy comes as easy as our lovemaking. To an outsider, it would look like we've been practicing at it for decades.

"First,"—I retrieve her clothes from the door—"let's get you dressed up."

"Thank you." Her eyes well up, as though she hasn't expected it.

Thoughts, the unkind ones, rise in my head at her emotional reaction. I could discount it to the intensity of what we've done, what we've shared. That, or that no one's ever treated her with the reverence owed to a goddess like her. And that pisses me off.

"Songbird." Her name is cherished on my lips when I kneel in front of her with her clothes in my hand.

"I am she." The glow emanating from inside her lights up the dark office, sneaking into my cold and not-so-lonely-anymore soul.

"For the rest of my days, I'll work hard to assure you you're my queen." Lifting one of her feet off the floor, then the other, I slip on her ruined panties.

She gives me a lopsided smile while tilting her bum up, left and right, to help me dress her.

"Nothing less than that." Before putting on her jeans next, I guide her hands to my shoulders to support her. "Always my queen. Always."

My eyes close for a second when she bends forward to raise herself from the chair, and her soft hands lean on my shoulders. Everything around her is real, natural, as it should be.

Who cares if the people we are or how we came to be together isn't conventional? It shouldn't. It doesn't.

"I love you." Her breath fans against my hair, touching me inside my soul.

The shame of what I am, the one I held onto for years, is being shed one layer at a time around this woman.

Then, with her hands up and mine working on settling her shirt over her head, I realize I'm not the only one harboring self-doubt.

I'll Be Watching You

"You're really okay with what I do for a living?" she asks.

Her head emerges through the neck of the shirt, her doubtful brown eyes searching mine.

A straightforward, honest reply such as *Of course* or *You don't even have to ask* won't suffice. They'll sound like I'm brushing her off. Moreover, it will rob me of the opportunity to know her better, and as a consequence, I won't be able to make her feel better.

Whatever brought on these misconceptions that whatever she's doing is wrong will be squashed by me. It might take a while, but when it comes to what's mine, my patience and persistence are infinite.

The color blue outlines her lips. I silently cover her in her sweater, topping it off by wrapping her in my jacket, then crouch down to be at eye level with her. I'm not bothered by the drop in temperature. All I care about is her.

"In case I wasn't clear before, I admire you for what you do." I plant soft kisses on the back of her palms. "Besides, it's a part of you, and it's not like you're hurting anyone. The opposite, you're the carrier of joy. I'm proud of you, proud to be your boyfriend. The real question is why would you think I wouldn't be?"

She sucks in a shaky breath, blinking a couple of times. A fat tear rolls from her cheek to her jaw. My lips catch it.

"Come here." Placing my palm on the small of Sloane's back, I beckon her to join me on the floor.

There's no second-guessing in her drop or in the way she allows me to readjust her into my embrace. I lean against the drawers set beneath the desk, bending and spreading my legs to position Sloane between them.

With her back pressed to my chest and my arms warming as well as shielding her, I whisper in her ear, "It's always a safe space for you around me. Talk to me, my love."

"I had a dream since I was a little girl of becoming an actress," she starts, shifting to snuggle closer to me. "I didn't even celebrate my third birthday when I sang to Mom and Dad in the living room, then performed entire monologues from Shakespeare or Arthur Miller when I started junior high. I'm an only child, you see, so they spent a lot of their time and energy supporting me however they could. They took me to acting classes and came to see me perform at school plays. Sometimes I was lucky to nail the lead, sometimes I had a smaller role, but they haven't missed any of them."

A touch of warmth seeps into my heart. I imagine a younger version of Sloane, ambitious and relentless to reach each mountain summit she set as a goal. Then my heart pinches a second later, remembering why I asked her about this to begin with, and I pull her even tighter into my embrace.

I'll Be Watching You

"My teachers gave me great feedback too, in high school then in acting school. I...I thought I could make it here on Broadway." She sighs, her hands squeezing mine. "But I didn't. I mean, I played in a show here or there as a replacement. Nothing stuck, though. I tried hard for two years, sleeping on Liberty's, my best friend's, couch when I couldn't afford rent." She shrugs. "I guess I'm not that special. Nothing remarkable."

Sloane, in her attempt to control the tidal wave of painful memories, pinches her eyes shut, shaking her head.

"Don't you ever repeat that." I grip her chin, forcing her eyes to open. "I won't allow you to talk that way to yourself. Acting is a competitive, cutthroat business and, from what I read, even successful actors spend years after years of rejection. I haven't seen you act—though I would be honored to—but if you got so much praise, then it must be a wrong place, wrong time kind of thing. This has nothing, nothing, to do with you or your qualities as an actress, do you hear?"

"Never mind." Her eyes cast downward to the floor.

I fasten my grip on her to force her to look at me, to see how genuine I am other than being the man who loves her.

"It's in the past." She sighs. "I look fondly on it, love and appreciate what was, but I don't miss the stage. Not when it led me to the career path, I ended up pursuing. I love it."

"That's my good girl." My lips and fingers caress Sloane's skin, the former stroking her temple, the latter her opposite cheek. "So why the doubts?"

"I…" She trails off, steeling her jaw and starting again. "I let other people get into my head. I'm proud of what I do, you know? I am. The men I dated, well…"

The vein in my neck pumps, a violent rush of blood surging through it. But she continues, so I respect her and shut my mouth until she's done.

"'Why don't you go back to acting, Sloane?'" The offensive words are reiterated by her in a ridiculing yet beat-down tone. "'You'll embarrass me when we go out with my friends, Sloane.' Or—and this is the one that had Liberty picking up the pieces of my sobbing ass and forcing me to remember I wasn't doing what I did for anyone but myself—A real wife-material would just agree to quit doing this…job, accept her allowance, and keep her mouth shut.'"

I flex my fingers that have traveled down to her stomach, the need to avenge her burning bright like a red flag to a bull. "Worthless pieces of shit. Worthless."

Maddened by the incompetence I felt by being unable to get my message across to her profile, I guide her body until her back is on the floor and

I'll Be Watching You

mine on top of her. Sloane sees it for the protective gesture it is, her eyes becoming a picture of adoration without a hint of fear.

"You have me now, you understand?"

Her nod is all she gives me.

"The next person to disrespect you, to look down on you,"—I bend until our noses touch—"anyone at all, I'm coming after them. I may not look like a guy who spends his days at the gym, but I assure you, when pushed, I can be as lethal as any of them. You're mine, baby, and no one will ever disrespect you."

"I know."

Sloane's trust in me is so complete that she spares me from telling her about what happened last year to prove my point. The story about how I choked a guy twice my size who thought Denver left an office party by herself is just going to wait for another day.

For now, I'm only Sloane's.

"You are the best part of my days, the star to my darkest nights, Sloane Ashby." I melt my lips to hers, conveying whatever words are too meaningless to communicate. "Have been from day one and will be to my dying day. Any job you choose, any hobby you go for, I'll be there to support and encourage you."

She wraps her legs around my torso, pulling my naked body to her dressed one, and repeats what she said before wearing a smile on her face.

Eva Marks

"I know."

CHAPTER NINETEEN
Sloane

My bed is eerily lonely this Sunday morning.

A big difference from yesterday, when it wasn't anywhere near this quiet.

After Emmanuel promised me the universe, got me the coffee he said he would, and called an Uber to take us to my apartment, nothing in my life felt nearly as empty as this bed.

He scooped me up like a doll the second I was out of the car and carried me to the elevator and up the stairs.

Without too many words, Emmanuel kept letting me know I was his queen. That he'd let nothing hurt me, that my life going forth was free of judgment. That abundance of acceptance and love was waiting for me on the other side.

And for a few hours, it truly had been this way. I'd been kissed, hugged, fucked, and loved so thoroughly that I honestly thought I might explode with sheer happiness or melt from the sheer bliss of it. Of *him*.

We eventually went to bed, me spooned to his chest, him with his lips nuzzled to the crook of my neck.

But that's where the sweet part ends. Because now I'm alone.

I can sense he left even with my eyes closed, my body still in the stages of waking up. There's this chill, this emptiness in the bed that wasn't there last night.

"Emmanuel?" My voice is groggy, my hand searching for him blindly.

Nothing. Not a *little songbird* back or the warmth of his lean body beneath my fingertips.

He's not in the room, not in the apartment. Again, it's a notion I have backed up by a stack of physical evidence. No scents of bacon, eggs, or toast reach from the kitchen, no coffee brewing, either. The water isn't running in the shower and there's no trail of soap fragrance wafting inside my bedroom.

Complete and utter silence.

It doesn't mean anything, I remind myself. *This is Emmanuel, and he loves you just the same.*

He didn't leave me. Didn't whisper all those sweet words just to backpedal the next day. It's not my Emmanuel, not the man I fell for.

I'll Be Watching You

This thing, us, it's new to him. Hell, any relationship that doesn't revolve around work is new to him. The fact that he opened up to me—to the *real* me—that he let me in, vowed to give me what he hasn't to any other woman before me, that's a huge feat all on its own.

I should be grateful. I should be understanding, give him equal compassion as he doted on me—like making sure the covers are tightly tucked around my body—but the sting of missing Emmanuel twists my heart.

With the backs of my hands, I rub my eyes, determined to put an end to being this spoiled. We have such a good thing going on, and I'm sure that I'll see him again today.

After all, breakfast is overrated. Whatever meal Emmanuel chooses to share, that'll have to be the most important one of the day.

I stretch my limbs, a sense of optimism washing over me. Slowly, I turn to the side of the bed where Emmanuel slept, eager to sniff his cologne and the scent of his body from the pillow.

"Holy…" My lips curl in an uncontainable smile.

He hasn't left me alone. Not really.

A mint-colored slip of paper I recognize as mine rests beside me, a couple of sentences scribbled on it in a man's handwriting.

Emmanuel's.

The somersault my heart is doing could qualify for the Olympic Games.

Impatient to wait for another second, I lift it to my eyes and read it.

My little Songbird,

There are three things I want you to remember today:

1. I will always come for you.

2. For years you've brought to life every fantasy I had. Today, it's my turn to repay you.

3. The word daffodil *stops it all.*

Love,

Emmanuel

In my bed, with my sheet scrunched at my hips, my hair a nest on my head, and my naked body on display for no one in particular, I think. I rack my brains for anything I might've told him, a desire he hasn't fulfilled yet.

I come up blank.

In the short time I've known Emmanuel, love, sex, and endless excitement have been filling my cup in a steady, constant rhythm. Nothing is missing.

Except…

There was that day I spied on him, the first day of what started as a crush on my mysterious neighbor, never to recover. It's when I recorded my stalker-meets-consensual-non-consent podcast, which was meant for my subscribers, but in truth, it

I'll Be Watching You

was really about me and my depraved needs for Emmanuel.

It's been an expression of my instantaneous and bottomless attraction for him, for the sick games we could play together.

Plagued by a million questions—such as how long will he keep up the stalker part, when will I get to see him, and what will he do to me when he breaks in, and most importantly how will he do it—I jump off the bed.

Lingering on them will ruin the fun. Knowing what he'll do, how, and when means goosebumps won't prickle my skin whenever the weight of the stalker's gaze lands on my back, that my breath won't catch in my throat when he breaks in here.

No, I definitely do not want to guess, question, or play detective in this one. I'm going to give in fully to this experience.

Today, I'm neither Sloane nor am I Seraphine. I'm just a girl in the big city.

That. Is. It.

And what would a girl in the big city do over the weekend? Go out to revel in the last decent weather days before winter hits.

The hairs at the back of my neck stand up straight, forcing me to hug my khaki bomber jacket tighter around my torso.

Although it's still November, the temperatures dropped significantly since the beginning of the month. But this Sunday evening, chill isn't to blame for the sudden shiver coursing through my body, of the ice running down my spine.

The eminent feeling of being alone in a dark alley on my way to my apartment building.

It's been like this the entire day, though nothing as close and present as the way it sneaks up on me now. The person watching me stopped being an observer who hides at a safe distance while stalking me.

He's ready to pounce.

The man who's trailed me on my visit to every store in the neighborhood, who's been behind me as I ordered one latte then the second one on my travels up north. He'd never left me alone, evading me even in the wide-open space of Central Park where I had my egg salad sandwich and later on my lunch in an organic food cafe on the Upper West Side.

I'd tried playing his game, feeling sexy when, between meals, I blended into the crowds who ogled dinosaurs in the American Museum of Natural History, then walked among art lovers at The Met.

He hasn't lost sight of me, not once.

I'll Be Watching You

It didn't matter that I purposefully wore clothes to help me blend in and look like everyone else. My unoriginal jacket, the matching scarf I wrapped around my long locks with the intention to hide them, and a pair of my generic light-wash jeans haven't been an obstacle for my stalker.

He's aimed his attention at me constantly, his eyes burning holes in my back.

I didn't have to see those blue eyes to know they were glued to me wherever I went. I *felt* it. Felt Emmanuel.

And now that the time has come, the grand finale closing in, I'm starting to wonder…

Is the person following me home, right now, the same man who tracked me throughout the day?

I thought I'd be excited, thrilled, when the hours of anticipation would culminate into *this*. Truth is, given that no one's around combined with the fact I have no idea what to expect, I'm terrified.

I'm all over the place in the dark, away from the bustling part of the street and out of people's sight.

Slowly but surely, the arousal that has accompanied me throughout the day shrivels into almost nothing. The thrill that has blossomed in my gut morphs into a chilling sense of trepidation.

What if Arnie came in to work on a Sunday and called Emmanuel about a new, exciting finding? What if he left in a hurry, forgetting to tell me he was hitting pause on our game?

Eva Marks

What if...

Oh, God, no.

What if something like that really happened and the man whose heated focus is settled on me now isn't Emmanuel?

My breath catches in my throat, my feet picking up the pace to the street corner leading to my block. I don't dare look back to check who's behind me, don't avert my gaze anywhere but forward.

Even though I'm out of the alleyway, have returned to relative safety by being surrounded by noises, traffic, and a few dozen people, I don't feel any less exposed.

I break into a run, sprinting past the three buildings that separate me from my home, my shelter. I almost knock out a blonde woman about my age who mutters, "Watch it," but unlike any other day where I would, today I can't bring myself to apologize or care.

When I reach the entrance, the newlyweds who live on the first floor push the door open. Asking them for help is an option, sure. On the other hand, I could be imagining this. It's not impossible that after a morning *and* afternoon of being tracked by my boyfriend, I don't have a grasp on reality anymore.

Emmanuel might have gone away or it's him. I don't know any of the alternatives for sure.

In case it's not him behind me, I'll make a scene and have someone call the police.

I'll Be Watching You

Equally worse would be—and Christ, the embarrassment *that* would cause me—I'll be clutching their shirts, begging them to call 9-1-1 or to fend off a ghost, an invisible stalker I made up in my head.

I'll either break Emmanuel's trust or become that neighbor everyone's whispering about for the near future.

No, thanks. Telling them anything other than *Hi* isn't an option.

I have no one except myself to count on.

An awkward, "Hi" slips through my lips as I press forward, not stopping to ask how they're doing in my rush to get to the elevator.

"Everything okay, Sloane?" Alena, the wife, calls me.

"Never better!" I yell without slowing down, already pushing the door leading to the flight of stairs when I see the elevator isn't on the ground floor. I can't wait for anything and anyone.

Whatever she wants to say to me is being cut by the heavy door slamming behind me and the pounding of my feet on the stairs. I make a mental note to apologize to her later. Preferably with Emmanuel's arm wrapped around me in that possessive way of his. When I'll be safe.

I'll call him once I'm sheltered in my apartment. Once I can breathe again.

Eva Marks

Other than the blood whooshing in my ears and my boots slamming against the stairs, the stairway is silent. No one's here.

Either I really sensed someone who wasn't there, or he got locked out of the building once the Jackson couple left.

You have this. You're okay.

My hand still quivers when I reach inside my purse, fishing for my key to try and unlock the door.

"Come on, come on," I say to both myself, and the stupid key that doesn't seem to fit anymore.

Eventually, I'm able to slide it in.

The sound of the lock clicking open rings like one of the most wonderful symphonies I've heard in my whole twenty-seven fucking years of living. I slam the door shut behind me, locking it back in place along with the two deadbolts I forced my landlord to install.

Then, and only then, I'm able to function again, to inhale.

I throw my bag to the floor, flattening both my hands on the door and bowing my head as I try to regulate my breath. Oxygen starts filtering in my lungs, soothing the effects the adrenaline had on me.

But something isn't right.

A cold gust of wind blows from the window at my back.

I don't remember leaving it open, that is the last thing I think about before a firm hand presses my

I'll Be Watching You

mouth shut, the other one gripping my breast so hard I see stars.

And I scream.

CHAPTER TWENTY
Emmanuel

When I told Sloane I'll always come for her, I meant it. No door, lock, or any kind of barrier is going to keep me away.

I will, however, later, warn her about leaving the window near the fire escape open.

"Shut up," I growl in her ear.

I'm uncharacteristically cruel, being turned on by it as much as I am by her fear. From how she looked over her shoulder throughout the day, how she did her best to evade me.

Add to that the fact she had no idea where I'd been, and I'd been fighting a hard-on for hours.

But even if I weren't into it, there's no way I'd be standing here, acting any different. I'd do anything for her, including exploring any kind of fantasy she has.

I'll Be Watching You

Knowing she's into it is the only incentive I need. Even if it involves ripping me out of my comfort zone like today, forcing me into the role of the participant as well as the voyeur.

And yeah, I fucking love it. My raging boner pushes against my jeans, my cock jerking at the sound of her whimpers.

Her body slumps by some, though, when she realizes it's me. I'm not having it. We both want this, so for her to be fulfilled, for me to maintain the attacker act, she has to play along.

I breathe in her ear, pushing her to the door. My erection presses to her ass, my hand still blocking her mouth.

"I'm not Emmanuel this evening," is the only warning I give her before squeezing her breast harder while at the same time biting on her earlobe to get my point across.

Her shriek reverberates on my palm, the panic setting my sick desires on fire.

"You know,"—I move the hand from her tits to her stomach, dragging Sloane to the center of her living room—"I've had my eyes on you."

She cries helplessly when I throw her on the rug on all fours, trying to turn her head back.

"Do. Not. Look. At me." My growl scares her to face the gray fluffy yarn in front of her. "Not unless I tell you you're allowed to."

"I—"

"Don't say a word either." Kneeling behind her, I fist her scarf and tug. My lips return to her ear, my whisper is ominous. "I'm going to take what's mine and hurt you today, little girl. Any sign of disobedience will just make things much, much worse for you. Nod if you understand."

Despite the restriction, her head bobs by some. The sliver of moonlight casts a dim light on the otherwise dark room, granting me a view of Sloane's effort to swallow through the hold I have on her.

Her eyes are half closed, and her breathing comes out in short rasps of arousal I recognize from when I fuck her the way she likes.

"Greedy little whore." I release her without a hint of a warning.

At the surprise, Sloane's body slumps forward, her thick, burgundy tresses grazing the floor.

"I bet if I shove my fingers inside your pussy, I'll find it dripping, won't I?"

She begins to nod her head, straightening her arms to lift herself. I fling my palm on her ass. My brutal, unrefined force sends her to her forearms.

Then I wait. Because if this is too much, if she says her safeword and I don't hear it through the thunder of the smacks I'm about to land on her repeatedly, I won't ever forgive myself.

Aside from her labored inhales and exhales, nothing about her demeanor signals for me to stop. So, I don't.

I'll Be Watching You

I go at her for three painful smacks. *Slap, slap, slap.*

Sloane's choked groan is the only sound I hear in the aftermath.

I back away, sitting on the couch to have a good view of her, then command, "Get up and strip for me."

Her hesitation gets her retribution in the form of me leaning forward, gripping her waist and spanking her. I attach each word to a blow on her ass cheeks and the back of her thighs, saying, "You. Will. Do. As. You're. Told. Immediately."

"Oh!" she cries when I'm done and back on the couch, but begins standing on shaky legs and corrects herself by saying, "I'm sorry."

"I don't give a shit about your apologies."

Acting like an asshole and talking like one are two different things, and in this game, one doesn't go without the other. I'm fully aware it's just a character, a scene we're playing in. When it's all over, I'll love her like I always have all over again.

"Spin to me, eyes to the floor, and take your fucking clothes off already."

While she teeters on her feet to comply, I cross a line in the sand. I whip out my cock, stroking the length of it as I sit there, watching her undress and stroking myself without asking for approval or seeking it in her eyes.

Just because I fucking want to.

She eyes me momentarily, her gaze darkening by my actions, then quickly returns to the floor. Her jacket goes first, revealing a gray cardigan she pulls over her head.

The lust transforms into fear after that. It remains visible even in the dark, visible even when she doesn't look at me. It's in her parted lips and kneaded eyebrows I see from my vantage point on her couch.

"Your shirt, now." I take my time running my hand up and down my length, pretending to not care about her feelings. "You've kept me waiting long enough today."

Her quivering fingers grasp the hem of her gray, long-sleeved T-shirt.

"What part of *now* don't you understand?" My sharp tone comes off as a whip, coaxing a startled cry out of her. "Faster."

Gone is her shirt, the last piece to shield her modesty. Sloane's hands are balled into fists at her sides. I push up to stand, closing the distance between us in two steps. My free hand winds into her long hair, pulling on the roots.

"I'm pretty sure I was clear the first time, but I'll give you a courtesy reminder. I said,"—the skin on her neck breaks in goosebumps, responding to my teeth scraping along it—"strip. For. Me. Everything goes off. *Everything*."

I'll Be Watching You

"Please," she begs, and my dick jerks at the misery and trepidation painting her voice in terror. "Y-you don't have to do this."

"I warned you." I suck on her flesh, marveling at her scream. "What would happen if you disobeyed me."

"I'm sorry." Each syllable has a different lilt to it while she obeys, her fingers trembling as they move to her back to unclasp her bra.

"You just don't listen, do you?" Reaching back, I slap her hands away. "Fuck"—I yank the right strap down her shoulder—"your"—left one—"apologies."

At the end of the sentence, I shove her bra cups to reveal her breasts.

"But—"

"On your knees." Using the hold I have on her hair and the pressure I apply on her shoulder, I force her to the floor.

"No, please." Precum wets the tip of my cock at the horror in her eyes and her feeble attempts to wrestle herself away from me.

Whoever told her she's a bad actor doesn't know shit. From where I'm standing, my poor victim's fear is very fucking real.

"Begging won't help you." I slap her cheek with my cock once she's bent beneath me. "You're gonna suck it, Sloane. Trust me when I say this, you don't want to see what happens when you don't."

CHAPTER TWENTY-ONE
Sloane

"**N**o!" I scream before clamping my mouth shut, shaking my head and the rest of my body to try to wrangle myself from Emmanuel's hold.

His fingers are still tangled possessively in my hair, my chin locked in place when he grips it tight and pulls it down to coerce my lips to open. Emmanuel's thick cock stands erect in my face, ready to be shoved deep into my mouth.

I should be terrorized. The way he's been speaking to me, his behavior since he attacked me from behind, it's nothing like the man I know. Most of the time. There was a short moment when he paused—I'm guessing to wait and see if I safeworded.

It was there, then it was gone.

And I mean yes, we had rough sex so far, but it was never this violent.

I'll Be Watching You

But it's exactly what I want. On my knees, degraded, forced, and terrorized, I have never been more turned on. Never been more in love.

Which is why I fight him, pushing back with everything I have.

"Poor little girl thinks we're negotiating." Instead of pulling on my hair again, he lowers his hand down until he's curling his fingers around the back of my neck, using the leverage to shove me forward.

My lips and nose press to his shaft, to the pulsing vein and the silky, taut skin.

"Open up," he growls, rubbing himself on my face.

Behind my sealed mouth, I scream the word, "No!"

"Last chance." His menacing voice ignites panic in my heart and a searing fire between my legs.

The third *No* I mumble sounds far weaker, but I refuse to open my lips. I'm his victim, an unwilling one who will fight him to the very end.

It's then that I decided that he's no longer Emmanuel in my eyes. For the scene to go just right, he's now my anonymous assailant.

He pulls me back, cocking an eyebrow. The answer is still a muffled no.

"Suit yourself."

A fraction of a second doesn't pass from my attacker's final threat to the point where his thumb and forefinger clamp on my nose. He drives my head forward until my lips are smashed against his dick, cutting off my airways without a shred of mercy or consideration.

My eyes tear up at the unrelenting pressure my attacker maintains on my nose, but he doesn't care about that. Steel blue icicles glint at me from the dark above, making their intention known.

He's going to go through with it.

At the dawning realization, my nipples pebble and my breasts swell. The damp spot between my thighs pulsates as if it's its own living entity with its own beating heart.

"What a fiery little thing you are." He grinds forward to suffocate me further. "Too bad it won't do you any good. It's only a matter of time before I take what you refuse to give. You will choke on my dick tonight. Just a matter of time."

I remain firm in my denial for as long as possible, until the darkness surrounding Emmanuel's face becomes black, blurry spots.

Then I open up.

"Good girl."

The praise is tainted by the malevolence in his voice, spoiled by the speed with which his thumb latches on to the bottom set of my teeth to drag them lower, keeping my mouth agape.

In the haze I'm in, I think the man towering over me will thrust his thick, throbbing member past

I'll Be Watching You

my lips. He made it clear that's what he's after, that it's the reason he's been suffocating me.

And yet he doesn't.

He bends to me, his face inches from mine. I smell mint and coffee on his breath, see the cruel and sick desire in his gaze that has me panting against my will.

"But not good enough," he growls. "Because a good girl would've opened the fuck up, would've shut up to let me have my way with her. You, on the other hand, fought. I promised you you'll pay for it, and you will."

The person who stalked me all day gathers saliva in his mouth. I panic and sway toward him, my mouth watering with need while I work my jaw to try and clamp it shut.

He doesn't act like he's paying attention to any of it, to anything I do. I'm a vessel for his pleasure, for him to abuse. I'm a hole that he keeps open long enough for him to spit in.

"Yes." His satisfied grunt reaches my clit, my pussy, my heart. His next whisper, that one claws right at my soul. "Pinch my leg since you can't safeword, my dirty piece of ass."

I want to swallow it, have every bit of him inside me, but I resist. There's so much of his saliva in my mouth, on my tongue, dripping lower to my esophagus that I begin to cough.

Eva Marks

Instead of staying to admire his handiwork, how this part of him fills me, causing me to splutter and gag, the man straightens fast. Not wasting another moment, he grabs his dick, aiming the glistening tip at my forcefully separated lips, shoving it inside.

The girth of him stuffs my mouth, hitting the back of my tongue, and I part gag again, part moan with desire.

"Take it, you filthy whore." Harsh pummeling into my mouth accompanies his words, a glint of evil painting his tone. "Take every inch of me. I want to feel my spit coating it and your pretty little throat choking on it."

As if on cue, my pants of lust and struggle for air shorten, crack, and morph into sounds of retching.

"Fuck." He clutches his fingers at the back of my head, fucking my face ruthlessly, making tears stream out of the corners of my eyes. "That's it, little fuckdoll, cry for me while you gag on this big, fat cock."

My confusing yet unquenchable arousal has me bursting at the seams, my orgasm building up inside of me. I'm almost there, so close as I swallow on the thickness of my attacker, but I'm only close, never really there.

In my maddening desperation—where I float though I'm leashed to this man who fucks my face, where I'm more his, than I am my own—I seek for relief. I slip my hands lower beneath my navel,

I'll Be Watching You

blindly searching my waistband to undo my button and unzip my jeans.

"Oh, hell no." My mouth is left empty before I manage to do anything.

Cold and ruthless blue glare meets me at eye level when he kneels in front of me, pinning me in place when his hand cups my pussy like it's been his all along.

"Betrayed by your own greedy cunt, aren't you?" He finds my hair again, pulling to bend me backward, his teeth finding my left breast and sinking into it, hard.

"A man you don't know," he says between biting and sucking my nipple, between squeezing my pussy through my jeans. "Breaks into your house, humiliates you, violates your mouth, and you what?"

Spit from both him and myself is smeared on my chin. My jaw goes slack from being abused for long seconds without a single pause.

His palm leaves my center, slapping my tits twice on one side. "And all you can think about is masturbating. I guess I'm taking it too easy on you."

I've never had it so rough and so good in my life. I don't say it, however. I embrace the tears, tap into the degradation and abuse I went through, and I sob.

"P-please, please stop it."

"You'd like that, wouldn't you?" In strong, swift movements he spins me, then tackles me from behind and pushes me to the rug on my hands and knees.

"Please," I beg again, my chest heaving, legs trembling.

Emmanuel's, not the stranger's, gaze roams across my features. I recognize it's him from the way he's checking in on me through his eyes, even when he's silent.

My subtle nod grants me a, "Shut the fuck up with your *please*."

He leans some of his weight on me, using one hand to unbutton and unzip me. With a ruggedness matching his behavior throughout the night, he straightens to yank them down my thighs, taking my panties with them.

A whoosh of leather follows after he rids himself of his clothes. "Let's see how much you want to come now."

Smack.

This isn't the stinging of his palm. This is a torch branding the tender flesh of my ass over and over again. Powerful blows meant to inflict pain over and over, to debase me until my sobs are shrieks and cries and my body turns into a living wire, feeling everything all at once.

But after six of those, three on each cheek, when it's just trying to control my tears and my attacker breathing hard at my back, I'm transformed into

I'll Be Watching You

something else. I'm not merely sensitive, I'm flying so very high, right up there in the heavens.

"You're more broken than I imagined." He smacks me twice more on each cheek. "I can work with that. There's always another part to ruin."

"No!" My scream comes out as a breath, a huff of air rather than a word.

"Yes," he replies coldly, completely detached.

Silence ensues his warning. I'm tempted to twist my head, see what he's doing, though a second later I realize there's no need for that.

Not when three of his fingers penetrate and hook inside my pussy in one relentless, soulless shove. The cry leaving my throat echoes with the sound of my juices as I'm being pounded into.

I clutch the rug ahead of me, another feeble attempt to escape. I make it half an inch forward.

"Where do you think you're going?"

Slap.

This time, though, his hand doesn't leave the side of my ass for another round of spanking—his dull fingernails dig into my flesh, forcing me to remain in place.

"You're just asking for trouble, aren't you, little Sloane?" His fingers no longer fill me, now that my ass is being slapped with his dick.

"No, no, no." I'm lost between what's real and what's not, floating and grounded, yet not a tiny bit scared.

"Too bad." The blunt crown of his cock parts my swollen folds, positioned at my entrance, prepared to take me. "Because you're getting it anyway."

I expect my pussy to be ripped, for his long shaft to impale me all the way to the hilt. What I do not expect is three spit-coated fingers to sink into my other tight hole at the exact same moment he does that.

Stars cloud my vision, a million waves surround me from above, below, and sideways, causing me to undulate back and forth to their demanding rhythm.

It takes me the whole of a minute, or maybe ten, to descend a fraction from subspace and be in this living room with him. To realize my house isn't an ocean, my floor hasn't been flooded by the salty water of the sea.

What's pushing me, rocking me, splitting my world in half to give me a glimpse of just how good hell would feel like.

"That's it, little fuckdoll." He slams into me from behind, his balls slapping to my wet flesh. "Lie there and take this cock like the meaningless hole you are."

His crassness thrusts me higher and higher again while winding me like a string that's about to snap. But I won't come, won't step out of character and make it look as though I'm enjoying this. Not unless he forces it out of me.

I'll Be Watching You

He drives into me, marks me, ravages me, owns me even when playing this evil stranger. The hand on my ass moves up to my hair, his fist pulling my head back to help him ride me harder.

I feel him swelling inside me, hear him cursing, and it's not long until his hot cum shoots into what must be my womb, he's so deep. It's visceral and erotic, to be used like this for his sole pleasure, and I almost climax from that alone.

"Baby." He suddenly pulls out before I manage to understand we're done. His hands stop being rough and transform into a silk touch caressing my back and hips. "My beautiful baby."

Emmanuel guides me instead of manhandling my body, flipping me gently onto my back on the plush rug. His blue eyes are tender, loving; his palms pushing my legs to the sides are gentle and kind.

"What are you doing?" I murmur at the sharp shift in his behavior, eyeing him kissing his way down my collarbone, tits, my navel ring.

"The scene is over and, fuck, you took it so well." His lips taunt my hood, his hands spreading me wider for him. "The only thing missing is for you to come into my mouth, little songbird."

With these words he starts licking me slowly, sucking on my clit, going lower to enter me using his tongue. He repeats these motions again and again, and somehow, this sweetness, this softness in his ministrations is just what I need to come.

"Emmanuel," I gasp his name for the first time today while pulling his head closer and spasming all over his face.

After I'm thoroughly done, he rises back up, kissing every tear streaked across my cheeks. Emmanuel tugs off the throw blanket from my couch, hugs me tight to his warm body, whispers words of praise and encouragement.

He knows what I want and knows what to give me without me needing to articulate it. Emmanuel's endless care is what will make me remember this scene we enacted for hours over this windy Sunday as one of the best days of my life.

"I love you so much, my little Sloane."

"I love you too, always."

In my soulmate's embrace, safe and cherished, my eyes flutter shut, my heart resumes its regular, slow pace, and I fall asleep.

CHAPTER TWENTY-TWO
Emmanuel

There's a battle of ownership going on in my heart and every living thought surging inside of my head.

One of the sides tugging for my attention is my job. I've lived for science for over two decades, consumed and thriving on the help I can offer others through it.

It fascinates me, intrigues me, gives me purpose. And it's more than that; if all goes well, someday in the near future our research will provide millions of people who lost hope with their quality of life.

And now with Arnie's team *this* close to wrapping up the discovery stage they've been laboring over, I'm even more drawn to it. Because once done, they'll advance to the preclinical trials. Then it's reaching for the moon, figuratively.

I'm invested in every project running in our labs, but this one, on the verge of a breaking point…

Fuck. Under any other circumstance, it would've been my everything. I would've stayed late nights, run the tests with Arnie's team.

Would have pushed him to do another ten just to be sure. Just so it won't fail so that nothing would've hindered us from—as much as possible—smooth sailing ahead.

Accept this isn't any other day.

While I'm at the lab, my woman is expecting me at home.

She hasn't told me her work was done for the day or anything like that—that's not what has me locking my office behind me at fifteen past six this evening. It's a feeling. Something in our connection tells me she's finished recording her podcast and waits for me.

For me.

Me.

She doesn't need to say it. It's been laid out for me all throughout the day, in how quick she picked up when I called her during my lunch break, in the smile I heard in her voice, her genuine interest in how my Monday morning was going.

It was even how her tone became husky and wanting after I told her I'm hard thinking about her, how she touched herself on my command, how she came with me.

That's why, even after the radio silence between us since lunch, I know she loves me as much as I love

I'll Be Watching You

her. She's the other aspect pulling at me for my attention, and yet she'll never demand me to choose. Sloane saw what my work means to me, and she respects it.

Fuck, I want her.

As I hold onto the handgrip in the subway, crammed with tons of people during rush hour, I have no regrets of walking out of the office earlier than I normally would have. The smells, noise, and commuters don't bother me either.

I'll be in my living room soon, watching Sloane for several minutes in the dark to sate my need, then walk over there and fuck her with her ass high and hands grasping at the coffee table.

The subway ride finally ends. I get off at my station, bracing for the wind whipping at my face the moment I climb the stairs and out to the street. Avoiding the fallen leaves scattered on the sidewalk, I head to my apartment building.

I open the front door, but before I go in, I look up at the window facing my living room. The lights are on in Sloane's apartment. If I don't want to get caught, I'll have to be extra cautious.

Which isn't that hard. I switched off every lamp and light source in my home before leaving this morning. The darkness surrounding me when I enter allows me to drop my bag and keys and move stealthily toward the window.

Eva Marks

My pulse quickens at the view I'm being given. Like I suspected, my girlfriend has finished her work for the day, sipping on wine with her back to the window, headphones in her ears, and leaning on the counter so her round butt flashes at me beneath her black shorts.

Another hunch—a pang of the bond we formed—whispers to me that she's doing it for my benefit. Just like I can sense other things about her, I'm sure she does too. She knew I'd be back at around this hour, or she could've felt me walking in. She simply did.

Heat courses through my body, my cock rock hard in my gray suit pants. My hands twitch to reach the top button, shove my hand inside, and stroke. Sloane wouldn't mind, and I'll tell her about it later. There are no secrets between us, and she did consent to it.

Except…

A movement at her door surprises me. At first, I think this has to be Liberty, her best friend. This may be a part of Sloane's game, giving me a view of her daily activities the same as she does on her vlog.

But then a tall, broad-shouldered figure enters her apartment. A man who must be around six foot one, wears his black hair cut short and his charcoal-gray trench down to his knees walks inside, his gaze aimed directly at Sloane.

I'll Be Watching You

A frown forms on my face, my eyes squinting, gauging who this person is who slips into my girlfriend's home. I study his self-possessed gait, how he let himself in like he belongs.

Recrimination and doubt flood my body when he shrugs off his coat, hanging it by the door. It's a gesture clearly pointing to how at home he is in her apartment. He's either been there before or she invited him.

Could this be happening again? Have I been a placeholder for someone else? Imagining our bond, our connection, the love she claimed to have for me?

My blood boils in rage and my head pushes me to turn away, close the drapes, forget Sloane ever existed.

To return to my safe, solitary life, where my success comes in the form of tubes and findings, and published articles. From curing mankind instead of being their puppet on a string.

My heart, though, needs me to get final proof. Once I see it with my own eyes, I'll be furious, break every fucking thing in this apartment down. I'll let her go.

So, I do what I always have.

I watch.

I watch the man coming into Sloane's line of view.

I watch the second it takes her to recognize him, zoning in on her reaction, then on her wineglass crashing to the floor. It splinters into a million tiny pieces, the red pooling around them like blood.

But I don't care about the glass.

Not when I see Sloane spin toward the window. Her eyes widen in horror, and though I'm unable to hear what she's screaming in my direction, I can read the words torn from her mouth.

They—along with the stranger who traces her steps, ready to pounce her—cause the vein in my neck to nearly explode, evoking a basal need to protect her that sends me whipping back to run to her place.

In my murderous, possessive need to defend what's mine, my body works on autopilot, my hand reaching to snap a butcher's knife out of its block on the kitchen island, my feet carrying me at rapid speed out of my house, to the stairway, into the dark street.

A distance that should be short stretches as if I'm on a goddamn marathon with how long it's taking me, made even longer by the tormenting memory of Sloane's words.

Words that'll torture me for the rest of my life if I somehow fail to save her.

Those two.

Fucking.

Words.

Help me.

"I'm coming, songbird."

CHAPTER TWENTY-THREE
Sloane

"**G**et off me!"

My assailant's grip—the real attacker, not my Emmanuel—tightens around my hair, tugging at it, not caring he's almost tearing it from the roots.

"You filthy slut." The stench of alcohol reeks from his pores, the pungent scent wafting directly to my nose as he pins his cheek to mine. "You think you can be such a fucking cock tease for years and stay safe?"

All I have to do is wait for Emmanuel. Emmanuel will be here.

At some point during the evening, minutes before my house had been broken into by this repulsive stranger, I sensed Emmanuel's gaze on me. The swelling and heat between my legs alerted me to it, then the goosebumps rising across my flesh told me he was definitely watching me.

When I turned to his window to cry for help, I saw him, too. Or more like his shadow. I was aware of what it might've looked like, given we'd enacted the exact scene yesterday, but I also knew that if I cried for him, he'd read this for what it really was.

And he did. His silhouette on the other side of the alley moved so fast; one second there, the next gone.

He's coming for you.

"There's no hiding, *Seraphine*," the man drawls my stage name, his disgusting lips and week-old scruff grazing my skin.

I bend my elbow as much as physically possible, hitting the asshole in the stomach. Any second I can buy until Emmanuel gets here is more than precious—it could be lifesaving.

"Fucking whore." He thrusts me forward, gluing the side of my face to the glass, pinning my arms to the front while pressing his evident and nauseating erection to my ass. "A million IPs pinging across the world aren't an obstacle if someone really wants to find you."

I just need to survive these few minutes, I repeat in my head.

This asshole gets off from my attempts to fend him off, judging by the hard dick he's grinding into me with each of my attempts to break free.

Further resistance or engaging him will only serve to worsen my position, might encourage this

I'll Be Watching You

cocksucker to stop his games and take what he wants faster than Emmanuel can get here.

"Then again,"—my belly is being violated by his unkempt fingers on his failed maneuvers to undo my cutoff button—"a whore like you, with your stalker, non-consensual type of podcasts, you're probably all too happy to be taken this way, aren't you?"

Through the fear I'm experiencing, rage splits through. What he's saying is a bunch of dinosaur-age bullshit. Any person has the freedom to choose their career, their partner, or their one-night stands. Now more than ever, I have zero shame in what I do for a living. It doesn't give anyone the right to force himself on me.

But despite floods of despise wreaking havoc on my body that urge me to do everything I can to hurt him in return, I remember Emmanuel will barge through the door at any minute. It'll be safer that way.

Be a smart girl, songbird, I hear his voice in my head. *Don't say a word to aggravate him. I'm coming for you. I'll always come for you.*

"Cat got your tongue?" The incompetent asshole manages to snap my button open, his hand slipping down my short zipper, continuing to shove them to the floor. "Don't play coy with me, *Seraphine*. I've been listening to and watching you for months. Tell me and only me what a desperate cunt you are, eager to take my cock up your ass."

The man's fingers curl around my panties, then tug in his intent to tear them right off. A tear of fury leaks from my eye, the one that isn't mashed into my window. I'm mad, so mad for myself, for the countless people who go through the terror I'm going through just because some maniac decides to release his cruelty on them.

He drives me to a breaking point, seconds from snapping. Fuck the consequences, what he'll do to me if I fail. I'll fight this fucking fucker and whenever Emmanuel gets here and however broken he'd find me, I trust that my love will piece me back together again.

However, neither I nor the asshole behind me do any of the things we planned on.

In my peripheral vision, I gauge a movement; a familiar man appears from the hallway and walks into the living room.

Emmanuel.

Air rushes into my lungs. Seeing my lover there, clutching a monster-sized knife, I'm not even bothered by the question of how he entered my home. I'm being given a new sense of mission, a need to fight, to help him.

I don't need to be a silent submissive anymore.

I need to be a distraction.

"Okay then, I'll talk." My eyes shift from Emmanuel, ignoring my approaching lover in favor of my would-be-rapist. Fortunately, my voice alone

I'll Be Watching You

puts some sort of spell on my would-be-rapist and he stops trying to tear my panties off. "I'll tell you how all my fucking life I've been yearning for a taste of a small dick like yours. Thank you for making my dreams come true, fucker."

"Stupid cunt, you'll get what's coming to you—" he starts but doesn't get to finish his sentence.

"I'd think long and hard about the next words your disgrace of a mouth is about to say," Emmanuel growls, menacing and a million times scarier than I'd ever heard him.

I couldn't imagine my boyfriend being more cruel, more harsh than he was with me yesterday. Clearly, I got it very, very wrong.

The pressure on my back disappears in a flash. The adrenaline keeps me standing upright, or else the shock, relief, and I would've stumbled back to land on my ass.

I recover fast, rushing to pull up my cutoffs, hiding as much of me as I can. Once I'm less exposed, I spin to the image of Emmanuel grasping the man's hair, my boyfriend's knife pinned to my assailant's bobbing throat.

"You want the whore too?"

The blade nicks into the flesh just enough to draw blood.

"We can share her!" he yells.

Emmanuel's blue eyes blaze in my direction.

I have you. I got you. I'll always come for you, they say.

He sinks the knife a little deeper.

A fat drop of blood creates a red streak on my attacker's Adam's apple, tainting his white shirt in a crimson splotch. Emmanuel is around three or four inches shorter than him, but he's undoubtedly stronger in his rage, maddened by his need to protect me.

"I said,"—Emmanuel grinds out every syllable through fiercely clenched teeth—"you'd better think about what you're about to say and how you talk to what's *mine*."

The three of us are in the eye of the storm, joined in a crazy, violent situation.

I'm not afraid, nor am I repulsed by the savage my boyfriend transforms into in front of my eyes. I'm turned on and more in love than ever.

"Yours?" The man spits. The only thing I notice is how the saliva is ruining my rug.

It makes me want to kill him all the more.

Maybe that's why I don't find it in me to feel sorry for him when Emmanuel jabs him harder.

"You're not a smart motherfucker, are you?" Emmanuel kicks the man behind his knees, coaxing a shriek out of him and forcing him to the floor. "But you'll learn. You'll learn to never touch her or another woman ever again. Not from your place behind bars. Call the police, songbird."

I'll Be Watching You

"You can't do that," the other man growls. "I'll tell them *you* were the one who attacked her. That I heard a noise, tried to fend you off, but your skinny ass somehow outmaneuvered me."

"He really is an idiot," I tell Emmanuel. A manic smile tugs at my lips, my finger pointing at the camera I left earlier on the coffee table. "See the red dot over there? Em, help the poor guy look, please."

Emmanuel's eyes and teeth flash in tandem when spinning the other guy. I guess the adrenaline has us both a tiny bit crazed.

"Long story short, since it's none of your fucking business." Crouching beside the man whose squinting eyes are meant to scare me, but in fact, do nothing at all. "After I was done with work, I left this on for my boyfriend, to record my evening, especially for him. So, asshole, you can lie all you want. The truth is right fucking here. Recorded."

"Bitch," he grunts without an ounce of fight in him while his throat still bleeds.

For that comment, he gets his kidneys kicked by my hero.

"Call the police, songbird," Emmanuel repeats in an authoritative voice, one that leaves no room to oppose him. Not that I want to.

On quivering legs, I tread to my cell phone in the kitchen. Then I relay to the operator exactly what happened, and when I know that both

Emmanuel and I are safe, only then do I collapse to the floor, suddenly drained.

Careful not to cut my feet on the wineglass shards, I lean on the kitchen island where this horrible evening started, staring at Emmanuel. The weight of being attacked in my home barrels into my chest in a rush, as heavy as if the Empire State itself collapsed into it.

In this moment of mental exhaustion, I don't seek vengeance. I'm not turned on. I'm not anything but an empty shell, just like the bleeding man being held by Emmanuel intended me to feel.

An upheaval of tears rises, and they flow out, dampening my cheeks, my jaw, and my lips.

"Sloane." Emmanuel's lips make out the word, although I don't hear it very well. "Can you do me one last favor, beautiful?"

"Y-yes." I nod. I'll do anything for him, no matter what.

"Get me the rope from your room." My lover's command is softer now, though equally demanding. "Then I can comfort you."

Of course, he'll know I have them, and what a comfort it is. Driven by the need to be held by Emmanuel, I ignore my weakness, treading toward my room to retrieve one of the long ones I have and one of my scarves. Together, we tie up and gag the man I hope will rot in jail for many, many years.

I'll Be Watching You

"Come here." Emmanuel envelops me in his safe arms, leading me to the couch where he cradles me, sheathing me with every inch of his warmth.

"How did you get in?" I murmur into his chest, breathing in his cologne, his scent, and most importantly, him.

He huffs out a breath, shaking his head. "I forgot to tell you yesterday. You left the fire escape window unlocked."

"Oh." My fingers clutch Emmanuel's shirt, grasping into the blanket of security he embodies. "I thought you picked the lock somehow before I got here, that's why I didn't lock the deadbolts today. I'm so goddamn stupid. So irresponsible."

"Shh, don't you dare say it." Heat pulses through me when he kisses my hair, pulling me deeper into his hold. "You didn't ask for it. No one ever asks for it. Rest until the police get here. I have you. For as long as I live and even after that, I will always have you."

CHAPTER TWENTY-FOUR
Emmanuel

Not too long after Sloane called 9-1-1, the police arrived at her apartment. The two officers who made it there first handcuffed Sloane's attacker—whose name we discovered was Ron Fortin—followed by a CSI and two Special Victims Unit detectives who entered the scene.

The motherfucker I was inches from killing was hauled into the back of the squad car. After that, the officers pulled me aside for questioning away from Sloane as they weren't sure yet that I hadn't been Ron's accomplice. They were professional and to the point; moreover, when provided with proof, then they cleared me.

Their help and efficiency played two big roles in reassuring Sloane justice would be served. None of them acted judgmental toward her and her

I'll Be Watching You

profession, not once blaming her for the—as Ron said—asking for it.

The SVU detectives, a man and a woman, made sure to emphasize it, too, and I believed it was them who helped her to relax the most. Ceding control over Sloane to others got under my skin, so much so that I had to clench my fists instead of opening my mouth to relieve her from reliving the whole story and leave the rest to the tape.

She was mine to look after, mine to protect.

But I wasn't an idiot to not realize the importance of having a professional console and talk her through the traumatizing event.

She needed it, which meant I had to shut up and let them do their job.

She'd still need the time and space to recover, and she'd do it while the police had every word and all evidence to have their case ready for court. In my arms, under my web of protection.

No one, not one fucking person, will ever look at her and much less touch her in a way that violates her again.

Years of learning self-control helped me restrain myself from propelling into some sort of action. I crossed my arms over my chest, leaning one hip on Sloane's living room wall to hover without butting in.

Spirals of fury, pain, and need for vengeance unfurled in me hearing her retell what happened, how she felt in those minutes I hadn't been there. How shocked then terrified she'd been when Ron let himself in the apartment, how he allowed himself to touch her like she was public property and partly belonged to him.

How he'd been moments from taking and hurting what's *mine*.

I bit the inside of my cheek in an effort to not curse out loud, digging my fingers to the inside of my palm to stop myself from doing some serious damage to the flower vase at arm's reach.

The detectives, Leona and Maurice, reassured her repeatedly this wasn't her fault, treated her as tenderly as one would a soap bubble they tried their hardest not to pop into thin air. Eventually, the color returned to Sloane's cheeks, the tears stopped streaming. Even from three feet away, I could sense her pulse begin evening out.

"Em?" Sloane's voice drags me from my thoughts.

Whereas it'd usually bring a smile to my face, this time, seeing her this vulnerable, it does not.

I look around us at Leona and Maurice who stand up; their job is done for the night.

"I'm here." I lower to the couch right next to Sloane, curling my arm around her to pin her to my side. "Always will be."

I'll Be Watching You

"As we just told Ms. Ashby," the tall, long-haired Leona says, "we covered most of the bases tonight, though it'll be a while before we're done."

Common courtesy calls for me to rise to my feet, shake their hands, thank them before showing them out. I don't. I've kept my distance from Sloane long enough throughout their interview. Being polite isn't a blip on my radar, not when I don't plan on leaving her again anytime soon.

"Thank you," I say, though my attention is firmly fixed on the woman I'm cradling into my body. "You have our numbers if you need us."

The other detective, who's about five inches shorter than his female partner and twenty pounds heavier, flicks his gaze between us. "We also ask that you don't travel outside the state in the meanwhile."

"We won't," I fill in. Sloane has talked plenty for one evening, no use to exhaust her further. "But she won't be staying in this apartment either."

"I won't?" She stirs in my arms, her bronze gaze cast upward to mine.

I work out in my head an explanation that won't result in me sounding like a controlling dick or a primitive *Me Tarzan, You Jane.*

"It's safer that way."

"I'll lock up better next time."

A strand of her soft hair drapes on her forehead where a bruise starts to form. A swollen, red bump that son of a bitch caused by smashing her profile to the window.

I tuck her lock carefully behind her ear, kiss the tiny hill on her head, reminding myself the kind of firmness Sloane needs is the gentle one.

"We'll be heading out," I hear Maurice saying in the far, faraway distance.

Because in this apartment, in this universe, there's no one but Sloane and me. The door shuts, a dull noise echoing somewhere around us.

"It wasn't your fault." I repeat the sentence I'll keep telling Sloane until there's no shred of guilt left in her. "He's a sick, violent person who shouldn't even be allowed to breathe."

It takes great effort to hold my gaze to hers. I'm aware of what and who I am, of my own depravity. I'm cognizant of my lurking and stalking tendencies. Of being turned on by watching a woman who can't sense my presence, at least anyone but Sloane.

Then my little songbird talks to me through her huge, deep eyes. Even weakened, she gets what's going through my mind, promising me I'm nothing like that. Reminding me I've been conquering it since day one.

With her silent reassurance, I continue.

"His weapon, one of many, is to blame his victims, shaming them. It's just another method of extending the torment." Every word is pronounced in a slow and calculated measure, in a dominant

I'll Be Watching You

voice that'll ensure the information sinks in. "All you've done is live your life, do the job you're passionate about, wait at home for the man who loves you. The rest is on him. And he will burn in hell for that."

No word is said between us after that for a while. When Sloane speaks next, her tone emanates confidence, unlike her question. "Are you sure you want me to move in? I'll be there. With you. Morning to night. On weekends."

Resuming the muted conversation our eyes were having, I understand what she's trying to convey to me.

"My love."

I slide my hands down the sides of her neck, her arms, grasping her waist and picking her up in the air. She yelps, though not in fear. With love. Her fingers find their way to my shoulders and interlace around my nape, her body melting into mine.

"You'll be surprised to know there are plenty,"—we pass her hallway, entering her bedroom—"plenty of methods for me to stalk you. To study and observe your every move."

"But won't you—oh!" Her adorable cry of surprise reverberates in the room when I dump her on the bed. "Won't you get bored?"

"Of you?" I cock an eyebrow, shucking off my jacket and rolling my sleeves up my forearms. "Impossible. Never."

Despite what she went through tonight, Sloane presses her knees to the sides, opening her legs for me. There's nothing seductive to the movement, not intentionally.

It's surrender, a plea to take her. A whisper telling me who can really make it better, who'll set her free by taking charge.

Me.

"I own you." On the surface the declaration sounds simple, plain, and yet it isn't. It's a promise I make, a vow to never let anything bad happen to her ever again.

I bring Sloane's knees together, leaning with one hand on the bed, the other on her jeans button to give her time to tell me whether she really wants it now or not.

"Please," she whispers. Her palms face down flat on her bed sheets, another gesture of complete surrender that has me hard and wanting. "Please, Daddy. I need this. I need *you*."

The verbal consent finalizes it for me. Meticulously, I slip the button out of its hole, unzip Sloane, and with one callous tug and remove both cutoffs and underwear off her.

"Sit and take your shirt off."

Sloane's obedience is immediate, her submission unwavering as she gives in to me by doing as I say, then whipping off her T-shirt. Without a bra on, she remains naked.

I'll Be Watching You

Beautiful. Perfect.

My woman.

"You know why, despite the fact I don't think I can be changed, you'll never, ever bore me?"

"Why?"

A rumbling *smack* slashes the air after my palm connects with her thigh. Two subtler ones come right behind when I slap Sloane's pink, taut clit.

Her shout and moan mix into a symphony while she remains my good girl and doesn't move. I'm maddened by the need to fuck her, but don't stray from my plan to take care of her. Tonight and for the rest of our lives, it'll always be about her.

"First,"—I rub her sore mound, a soothing motion before the painful squeeze I apply to it—"I said it in the past and I'll repeat myself for however long you need me to. You. Are. Mine. I've never loved another, and for two years"—releasing her clit, I sink three fingers in her pussy—"I haven't even considered searching for another woman online. You. Belonged. To. Me."

As if I've been sharing her bedroom for years, I get up and turn to Sloane's dresser, knowing what I'll find inside it. Being the good girl she is, Sloane remains silent on her bed, not asking questions, letting me dictate what's best for her.

She's right to trust me. She was right to do it yesterday, was right to do it when she was almost raped. She's right to do it now. In fact, there won't be a moment when her trust in me will be misplaced. Never.

Because a short while after I put on the song "Call Out My Name" by The Weeknd, I have the item I've been looking for in my hands. Hopefully, after this, at least for tonight, the memory I'll leave her with will be the only one on her mind.

It'll cast away the filth who hurt her and let the man who loves, adores, and is entirely too obsessed with her claim every piece of her consciousness.

Me. Only me.

CHAPTER TWENTY-FIVE
Sloane

My attempt to remain passive and his blow up in smoke once Emmanuel faces me again.

Because I can't help but gasp at the sight of him, of what he has in his hands.

In the corner of the dimly lit room, surrounded like a cloud by sultry music and the darkness he blends into so beautifully, Emmanuel stands holding my roll of bondage tape in his right hand, safety shears in the left.

It's brand-new, hasn't been used by me. Yet.

I bought it thinking it was cute. Looking again, in his grasp, the correct word isn't *cute*.

It's feral. When Emmanuel yields it, his blue gaze sending ice to race through my veins, I understand how this tape isn't a fun thing to try on. Emmanuel transforms it into a weapon, a tool he'll yield to cast away the horrible events of tonight.

The warmth in my blood is instantaneous.

My defender.

He walks closer, his presence becoming the shield I need around me so badly. My throat tightens, my clit throbs, and I gasp again with immense need and gratitude.

"Songbird." The way he says this name accompanied by his strong presence looming over me serves to placate my nerves.

I'm whatever he wants me to be, docile and compliant and silent.

I'll make a sound only when he allows it, talk only when he tells me to. Emmanuel might not be an experienced Dom in real life—outside the scope of his research—but he acts the part as if he was born to do it.

Chances are he just needed the woman who was perfect for him to unleash this power, this innate tendency in him. And, thank the stars, this woman is me.

"Your safeword." He places the scissors beside me on the bed, close enough to him to reach easily, far enough to not harm me if I shift by accident.

Watching him unravel the black tape, I'm nearly paralyzed by the burst of arousal capsizing my entire body. I'm mesmerized by the lean muscles of his forearms working, by his deft fingers stretching the material with precision.

I'll Be Watching You

"What. Is. Your. Safeword?" His command to answer drags me out of the well of lust I've been drowning in.

"Daffodil," I whisper from parched lips.

"Good girl," Emmanuel growls. He bends to his knees on the floor, presses my ankle and wrist together, and begins to bind them together.

"See, little Sloane. Continuing our conversation in the living room,"—the focus on this man while he wraps me has my pussy wet and thighs clenching, but I know better than to come without his permission—"it wouldn't matter if we were stuck in bed for a year together."

Emmanuel's tone grows husky at the third layer he plasters to my body. He inserts a finger between it and my skin to see it's not cutting off my blood supply, gazing up at me for approval. When I nod, he picks up the shears, snapping the tape to move to my left side.

"It wouldn't change a damn thing." His hands are warm and alluring as he restricts me. "I wouldn't care either way if you were glued to me the entire day or not. My love for you doesn't have to be in the shape of following you around, snatching you to a side alley, gagging you, and fucking you raw against a brick wall. It's a fucking turn on, but as long as I have you, I don't care."

My teeth dig into my bottom lip so hard I almost draw blood in my attempt to silence my moan. This still isn't my place to be heard, not while my Dom speaks to me.

"In fact, I'd love nothing more than to share a bed with you. Have you sleeping while I beat off to your bare cunt, make it nice and wet before I pull you out of your sound sleep when I'm hard all over again."

His words are an intent, a promise, a jolt to my core.

"Either that or I'll hold off on coming, wake you up with my lips sucking your clit and my fingers stretching your little asshole as my fist pumps my dick. Then when you're seconds from coming, I'll stop to rise on my knees, demanding that you pleasure yourself." *Stretch, cut, snap.* "My eyes will be glued to the fast movements of your fingers when you chase that orgasm you're desperate for, and I'll rub myself long and slow, forbidding you to reach it until my cum marks your body from your pussy to your tits."

"Daddy," I moan, unable to keep quiet anymore.

"Now, tell me, songbird." Thriving in his signature darkness, Emmanuel pushes my knees to the mattress without acknowledging what I said. "How could any of that ever be boring?"

It couldn't, but I don't have a chance to voice my answer. Emmanuel descends on me, his mouth closing on my sensitive nub, his tongue swirling and flicking on it, coaxing me toward an orgasm.

I'll Be Watching You

"Sing for me," he grunts between my thighs, drags two fingers along my slit, then pushes them in up to his knuckles. "But do not come before I say you can."

I do, though this time it's very different from the first time he asked me to sing for him. My cries are those of not only pleasure; the resonance of my voice embodies the depth of our connection and my adoration toward him.

I tell him without words how I fell for him, how I'm fully placing my life, well-being, and safety in his capable hands.

His groans of approval undulate through me, creating the perfect storm to twist my insides, to almost send me over the edge.

"Please," I hum more than speak.

"Please, what?" The question is asked in the passage of time between the moment he leaves my clit and the one when his tongue swipes at my pucker.

What I felt earlier doesn't even begin to compare to the sensation of Emmanuel licking my sensitive hole while stretching my butt cheeks open with his hands. I'm bound, spread, submitting to Emmanuel's silent command of holding on to my orgasm.

I beg and scream all at once, trying to wriggle from this intense intersection where heaven meets the flames of hell.

"Use your words." He hovers over my drenched slit, his scruff slick from his spit and my juices.

Through a fleeting second of consciousness, I manage to squeak out the words, "Please, let me come. Please, I'm begging you."

"That's a good girl."

His praise has me clenching my fists, has me praying my nails piercing my skin will be enough to curve the imploding arousal. Just a little, just until he tells me it's time to let go.

Emmanuel presses his thumb to my clit; the elbow of his other arm juts to the side when he jacks off, while his tongue laps circles around my asshole.

"Come all over my tongue." His permission finally arrives, then his tongue plunges inside me, fucking my ass.

My scream of relief breaks me in half first, then the rest of my bedroom. Slowly, as I'm carried back home by Emmanuel's patient licking, my world resumes the patterns it held before Emmanuel turned me into a possessed woman.

"So obedient." When he straightens, his cock throbs in his fist, a salty bead gleaming. "So beautiful, pleasing me like that. Obeying me blindly."

I nod, telling him wordlessly that yes, I am, and yes, I'll be that for him forever.

"Spit on them, make them wet for Daddy." He shoves two fingers behind my teeth. I coat them with

I'll Be Watching You

spit, so much so that some drips down my chin, making his eyes flare.

"Yes, exactly like that."

"Thank. You." My chest heaves, too full of air to allow me to say the two words together.

"Do you feel mine already?"

At the edge of the bed, where my ankles are tied to my wrists, Emmanuel probes and sinks two wet fingers into my ass.

"Feel claimed? Owned?" He quirks an eyebrow, dangerously serious while he's stretching my tight hole. "Protected, too, my little songbird?"

"Yes." The slow rhythm of his thrusts into me shifts, becoming a fast, violent one, making my heart soar.

Emmanuel doesn't have to hear me articulate what I'm feeling, though. The man who's in control over me knows what he wants, what I want, and how to get these two types of wants and needs to align together.

In the most self-possessed, visceral way possible, he draws out his fingers and spits inside his palm to smear it all over his cock.

"Correct, my love. Now, relax your ass for me." With his forearm on the bed beside my head, he cradles my cheek, his fingers biting into my scalp and flesh while he positions the thick crown of his dick at my pucker. "You're going to take all of me now, then I'm taking you home. Your new home. Am I clear?"

Tears brim behind my eyes, but not because of the tip of his shaft opening me as he waits for my response. It's this love, this finality. He's everything I've dreamt of for years, and he's ripping himself out of the shadows for me.

"Yes, you are," I say dutifully, looking up at my dark prince.

"My beautiful girl." His long shaft pushes into me, inch by inch until the entire length of him is inside. "My beautiful fucking songbird."

The calculated pace he starts with doesn't last. The icy blue color of his eye's swirls before me, morphing into a darker, more sinister shade the faster he grinds in and out of me.

He claims me as his and I do as he told me to. I take it. I'm his. I'm the good girl I'm longing to be for him.

He pins my knees to my chest, and the front of his body to mine so his pelvis grinds against my clit, driving me closer and closer to another orgasm. The sensation of my climax pummels hard into me, nearly as hard as Emmanuel's dick in my ass, and I fight to not give into it with everything I have.

By pleasing him, I'm complete, I'm his. Nothing and no one else matters.

Emmanuel's all-consuming glare pierces me. Through it, he lends me the strength I need to be

I'll Be Watching You

obedient despite the visceral need pulling me in the other direction.

Then his words reach my ears like a tall glass of ice water for his parched woman, "My fierce little Sloane, come on my cock, now."

When I do, my muscles clench one last time in a sweet and painful spasm. My voice is lost, replaced by groans and grunts and whispered curse words.

I'm collapsing from the inside, but through my lover's intense gaze and how he growls, "That's my good girl," and, "Fuck, I love how your ass milks my dick," he magically puts me back together again.

Hot spurts of cum shoot inside me, filling me with Emmanuel, making me truly a whole, complete human.

"You did so well." He kisses my mouth gently as he slowly slips out of my body.

I miss his presence there, miss the completeness of our physical connection. I want to tell him, to ask him to put it back, to never leave me. I wish I could, and I will, once the emotional toll of today will be a distant memory.

"Don't worry, baby." His thumb smooths the creases I didn't know formed between my eyebrow, his clever eyes reading into my soul. "You don't have to say anything. This is just the beginning of our forever. You'll have all the time in the world. *We* will have it."

He lavishes what feels like a million kisses across my cheeks, neck, collarbone, continuing to every exposed patch of skin on my body.

"Whenever you need me,"—with a mixture of efficiency and softness, he cuts off the binding tape—"I'll always be there for you."

He massages my ankles first, my wrists second before bringing one of them to his lips. "Even when I'm at work. For attention, love, sex, or anything at all, come over or call me. I meant it when I said you're mine. Anything you need, you come to me, and you'll have it."

"Emmanuel." A single tear breaks free when I'm strong enough to say his name, praying for him reverently. "Thank you."

"Sloane." He lowers himself next to me in bed, pulls the covers on top of our naked, sweaty bodies, then cradles my back to his front, burying his nose in my hair. "I love you. Always have. From the first time I heard your voice on your podcast, I knew what a precious treasure you are. Each day that passes, each second I'm with you, I'm a stronger, better person. I'm never letting you go."

My lips curve in a lazy smile; my body sinks deeper into Emmanuel's embrace. He spins me to him, bringing his forehead to mine, slithering his hand down my waist to my hip to guide my leg to drape over his.

I'll Be Watching You

"I stated it like it's a fact, but truthfully, it's up to you. Now that you have the facts laid out, that you know everything about me, will you…"

His pause gets me to wonder, gets me to wish so fucking hard that his question will go beyond sharing a living space. I understand it sounds crazy, and yet *this*, this eternity I want to have with him, it isn't a result of euphoria or an orgasm.

It's love. All-encapsulating, never-ending, once-in-a-lifetime kind of love.

And though I'm yearning to have him ask the question and say yes, so anxious that I almost propose to him myself, I wait. He might feel compelled to propose after I suggest it, protective or compassionate to ask me for all the wrong reasons.

"I want to marry you."

His declaration shocks the hell out of me. I examine his somber expression, seeing just how serious he is about it. He actually means it.

"I want the whole package, songbird. I want to worship you from morning to night, to love you for the rest of my life, through the good days and bad ones. To have you in any shape you come. It's too soon, yes. I don't care, though. I'm not taking it back. That's how much I love you, how much I want it, and how badly I'll fight for you."

"Y-yes," I blurt out, still overwhelmed with joy.

More than overwhelmed, actually. After all, what is a fitting description for this perfect moment in time when all the shit that's ever happened to me gets thrown out the window and I'm being granted every wish I could have ever dreamed of?

"You'll marry me?" His eyebrows shoot up like he wasn't expecting me to say it.

"Yes." The second time, I sound confident, clasping at Emmanuel's bicep to show him I'm as dead serious as he is. "Yes, I'll be your wife, Emmanuel."

"And I'll be the happiest man to be your husband."

He kisses me; he hugs me, holds, and possesses me.

From now on, not only am I his, but he is also *mine*.

EPILOGUE
Emmanuel

I haven't heard from my wife all day.

Every workday for the past year we've either talked on the phone during lunch, had it together in my office or on a bench at a park nearby, or I fucked her until she was boneless and sated with my office drapes shut and my desk cleared of paperwork.

And today…nothing.

Her absence should've pinged on my radar way earlier than seven in the evening. Thing is, my schedule has been swamped with meetings due to Arnie's team taking their findings to the preclinical trials.

Lawyers, management, paperwork… I've been drowning in them.

Now, in the darkness and silence, I miss my wife.

Eva Marks

Sure, I could pick up the phone, be like any other husband and call her.

I could. And yet I won't.

If she hasn't called me either, I'm pretty fucking confident Sloane is eager to play some game. One where I break into our new and bigger apartment housing Sloane's larger studio, and take her any way I choose.

My dick gets hard just thinking about leaving the world behind in favor of living out my kinks while fulfilling my wife's fantasies all at once.

I leave the office, heading straight toward the subway on route to our home. The crisp air and autumn weather that used to enchant me now appear in many shades of gray, uninteresting and irrelevant compared to the bright rainbow of my existence that is Sloane.

A few stations later, I'm out of the subway, walking the several blocks it takes to reach our apartment building. Before I punch in the code to enter, I look up to our window facing the street.

The lights are off; the drapes are only partly drawn.

Any other man who knows his wife should be home, yet seemingly isn't, would've been suspicious.

Me? It feeds my hunger. She is playing a game tonight.

I'll Be Watching You

My dark desire claws at my chest, pulling me upstairs. To see her, to have her. To call her filthy names, spank her ass red, tie her and pound into her.

To hug her later and call her my good girl, my precious little songbird.

Unable to hold off any longer, I push the door and ride the elevator to the fourth floor. I don't climb the fire escape anymore to get to her. Since what happened a year ago, we make sure to lock the window even when I'm with her at home.

We upgraded the locks in the new place as well, so when I stand in front of the door to our apartment, I have to use my cellphone for the smart lock we installed as a deadbolt replacement.

It clicks softly, and I let myself into our home. After a minute of adjusting my eyes to the darkness, I hear her.

My songbird.

"Em."

I turn to the sound of her voice coming from our room. It's neither scared nor panicked, but it isn't sultry or joyous, either. It's cold, distant. In a split second, my desire and plans I might've had for tonight vanish into thin air.

"Sloane." I drop my bag and keys somewhere on the floor, darting into our bedroom.

"I'm here," she says, then adds, "I'm okay. I think."

By the time she finishes that ominous *I think*, I'm already kneeling by our bed at her feet.

The lamp on her nightstand is switched on low, the amber glow casting shadows on Sloane's pale face. Her hair is pulled up in a messy bun, and she's still wearing her pajamas from this morning.

"Baby." I take both her hands in mine, my eyebrows kneading together as the anxiety spreads through me like poison. "What's going on? What happened? Was someone here?"

"No. Well." Her hiccup is a sob and laughter combined. "Not was. Is."

I jump to my feet, my body steeling to become a firearm instead of something made of flesh and blood. "Where?"

"Em."

"Where. Is. He?" I growl, thinking of all the ways I'll bury the person who has my wife in hysteria, who plays cat and mouse with us right now.

"Em," she calls me again.

This time, I stare down at her. She holds up a small plastic stick in her tender hand, offering it to me.

"There's someone in *here*." Her free hand points at her navel while I try to make sense of what's standing there in front of me.

"You…?" The two blue stripes complete Sloane's message. "You're pregnant."

"We're pregnant."

I'll Be Watching You

I drop to sit on the bed, lifting Sloane to straddle me. My heart pounds through the most wonderful emotional rollercoaster I've ever been on. I don't know how it will ever stop.

She's been off the pill for two months, which shouldn't have been enough for the hormones to clear out her body. Shouldn't, but it happened nonetheless.

Thank God for huge miracles.

"Are you happy?" she asks between sobs.

"Happy is too bland of a word."

I thread my fingers in her hair, pulling her to me for a long, thorough kiss. I tell her in that kiss how much I love her, how she makes me the luckiest man alive, how I can't fucking wait until we welcome to the world the missing piece to our family.

"Are *you* happy?" Finally, I release her just a little bit, a space for her to tell me what she feels about it.

"You're right." She nods, kissing me again. "It is too bland of a word. It's everything you said without words just now, Em, it's exactly how I feel. I love you and our baby so freaking much."

One of my hands slides lower, from her face to her belly. I kiss my wife, then press my forehead to hers and say, "I love you two, too. Forever."

The End.

Eva Marks

I'll Be Watching You

About the Author
Writing edgy spicy novellas, addicted to HEAs, and an avid plant lady.

Stay in Touch!
Newsletter for new releases:
https://bit.ly/3c3K2nt
Instagram: https://bit.ly/3QQ3Nh4
TikTok: www.tiktok.com/@evamarkswrites
Facebook Group: https://bit.ly/3LnFpln
Website: https://www.evamarkswrites.com

Eva Marks

More Books from Eva Marks

Blue Series
Little Beginning, book #0.5
Little Blue, book #1
Little Halloween, book #2
Little Valentine, book #3

Adult Games Series
Toy Shop, book #1
A New Year's Toy, book #2

Standalones
Primal
Dad Can't Know
I'll Be Watching You
Obsession – Coming October 3, 2023

I'll Be Watching You

Obsession: A Dark Horror-Erotica Romance Coming October 3, 2023. Pre-orders are live on Amazon

I obsess over her. Protect her. And when she needs me, I'd Kill for her. Soon she'll see that. So will her enemies…

My goddaughter is *everything* to me.

I was her dad's best friend, which means I have *no* business wanting her the way I do. She's too sweet, too innocent for someone like me. So, I walked away after her parents died.
But I didn't go far.

I stalked her from the shadows, and it's a good thing I did. That's how I found out her so-called friends plan to rob her—of her virginity *and* her inheritance—before killing her.
They won't get the chance.
Every one of them is about to face this masked serial killer for the first—and last—time. I'll take them down one by one.

Because *no one* touches what's mine. And make no mistake…
Darlene Pierce is *mine*.

Printed in Great Britain
by Amazon